WAYLEN UNLEASHED

BROTHERHOOD PROTECTORS WORLD

TEAM KOA: ALPHA
BOOK FOUR

JEN TALTY

Twisted Page Press LLC

For the Dream Team. Thanks for taking this journey with me. You ladies rock!

PRAISE FOR JEN TALTY

"Deadly Secrets is the best of romance and suspense in one hot read!" *NYT Bestselling Author Jennifer Probst*

"A charming setting and a steamy couple heat up the pages in a suspenseful story I couldn't put down!" *NY Times and USA today Bestselling Author Donna Grant*

"Jen Talty's books will grab your attention and pull you into a world of relatable characters, strong personalities, humor, and believable storylines. You'll laugh, you'll cry, and you'll rush to get the next book she releases!" Natalie Ann USA Today Bestselling Author

"I positively loved *In Two Weeks,* and highly recommend it. The writing is wonderful, the story is fantastic, and the characters will keep you coming back for more. I can't wait to get my hands on future installments of the NYS Troopers series." *Long and Short Reviews*

"*In Two Weeks* hooks the reader from page one. This is a fast paced story where the development of the romance grabs you emotionally and the suspense keeps you sitting on the edge of your chair. Great characters, great writing, and a believable plot that can be a warning to all of us." *Desiree Holt, USA Today Bestseller*

"*Dark Water* delivers an engaging portrait of wounded hearts as the memorable characters take you on a healing journey of love. A mysterious death brings danger and intrigue into the drama, while sultry passions brew into a believable plot that melts the reader's heart. Jen Talty pens an entertaining romance that grips the heart as the colorful and dangerous story unfolds into a chilling ending." *Night Owl Reviews*

"This is not the typical love story, nor is it the typical mystery. The characters are well rounded and interesting." *You Gotta Read Reviews*

"*Murder in Paradise Bay* is a fast-paced romantic thriller with plenty of twists and turns to keep you guessing until the end. You won't want to miss this one..." *USA Today* *bestselling author Janice Maynard*

BROTHERHOOD PROTECTORS

ORIGINAL SERIES BY ELLE JAMES

BROTHERHOOD PROTECTORS WORLD

ORIGINAL SERIES BY ELLE JAMES

Brotherhood Protectors Hawaii World

Team Koa Alpha

Lane Unleashed - Regan Black

Harlan Unleashed - Stacey Wilk

Raider Unleashed - Lori Matthews

Waylen Unleashed - Jen Talty

Kian Unleashed - Kris Norris

Brotherhood Protectors Yellowstone World

Team Wolf

Guarding Harper - - Desiree Holt

Guarding Hannah - Delilah Devlin

Guarding Eris - Reina Torres

Guarding Payton - Jen Talty

Guarding Leah - Regan Black

Team Eagle

Booker's Mission - Kris Norris

Hunter's Mission - Kendall Talbot

Gunn's Mission - Delilah Devlin

Xavier's Mission - Lori Matthews

Wyatt's Mission - Jen Talty

Corbin's Mission - Jen Talty

Tyson's Mission - Delilah Devlin

Knox's Mission - Barb Han

Colton's Mission - Kendall Talbot

Walker's Mission - Kris Norris

Brotherhood Protectors Colorado World

Team Watchdog

Mason's Watch - Jen Talty

Asher's Watch - Leanne Tyler

Cruz's Watch - Stacey Wilk

Kent's Watch- Deanna L. Rowley

Ryder's Watch- Kris Norris

Team Raptor

Darius' Promise - Jen Talty

Simon's Promise - Leanne Tyler

Nash's Promise - Stacey Wilk

Spencer's Promise - Deanna L. Rowley

Logan's Promise - Kris Norris

Team Falco

Fighting for Esme - Jen Talty

Fighting for Charli - Leanne Tyler

Fighting for Tessa - Stacey Wilk

Fighting for Kora - Deanna L. Rowley

Fighting for Fiona - Kris Norris

Athena Project

Beck's Six - Desiree Holt

Victoria's Six - Delilah Devlin

Cygny's Six - Reina Torres

Fay's Six - Jen Talty

Melody's Six - Regan Black

Team Trojan

Defending Sophie - Desiree Holt

Defending Evangeline - Delilah Devlin

Defending Casey - Reina Torres

Defending Sparrow - Jen Talty

Defending Avery - Regan Black

*P*resley Miles smiled and waved to the passengers as they disembarked from the vessel *Liberty*.

"Thank you so much," the primary guest said, holding a thick envelope. "What a beautiful boat and what an incredible day. We're so glad we picked Driftwood Tours."

Presley preferred these small charters on the forty-five-foot catamarans over the snorkel tour boats, but just because she was the owner didn't mean she took all the high-tipping clients regularly. She needed to spread the wealth, even if that meant postponing paying off her ex-husband. "You're incredibly welcome. We hope you'll look us up if you're ever on Big Island again."

"Not only that, but we plan on telling all our friends. Hands down, this was the best day cruise we've ever been on." The guest placed the tip money in Presley's hand. "You're a great captain and the chef on board was fantastic."

"I appreciate that." Presley nodded. She stood on the dock and waited for the guests to get to land before turning and climbing aboard *Liberty*.

This boat was a beauty. A few years ago, she'd replaced two catamarans, which had given her an edge over the other local companies—something she desperately needed. Only, that had put her more in debt. Vernon had thrown a fit. Not because she'd bought the boats, but because she hadn't discussed the trade-in with him first. Well, it wasn't his decision. He might own part of the business, but he was absent most of the time. He wanted to collect a paycheck. That's how it had been since they divorced. When he did show up, all he did was give her a hard time about the decisions she made, citing his way would have been better.

Bullshit. The worst part was he kept proposing stupid ideas and booked charters when he wasn't supposed to, often offering discounts, cutting into her bottom line.

She peeked into the envelope and counted the bills. Nice. On day charters like this, there was a chef, one deckhand, who also worked as the stewardess, and herself. "Are you two ready to see what those nice folks left us?"

"Absolutely." Adriana, the chef, wiped her hands

on her apron as she stepped from the galley. "They were so much fun. Adorably sweet. I wish all customers were like that."

"Me too," Jeff, the deckhand, said, making room at the aft table. "They make this job worth all the rich assholes who treat me like their maid and personal boy toy."

Presley laughed. "This tip has to be the best one we've gotten all season." She yanked the cash from the envelope. "Three hundred apiece."

"You've got to be kidding me?" Adriana blinked. "That was generous of them for a day trip."

"Hey, boss, you've got an unwanted visitor." Jeff jerked his head toward the end of the dock. "I heard he's been giving you a hard time again."

"Again? He's never technically stopped. If it's not in person, he's sending me dumbass emails." The last thing Presley needed was a face-to-face meeting with her idiot ex-husband. She should have known he would break her heart and leave her with nothing but trouble based on his first name.

Vernon.

Who the hell falls in love with a man by that name? Sadly, she'd been smitten with a scam artist. She fell for his charm hook, line, and sinker.

What a fucking sucker she'd been.

"He'll have to go jerk off because we need to turn this boat over. It's going out at eight sharp for a

3

three-day rental with Bobby as captain and Tilly as deck. Adriana, you're the chef on that one."

"I heard the guests have never been sailing before and that this a bucket list trip for them," Adriana said.

"I've already got some good snorkel and fishing spots set up, but the sailing on the second day looks like the wind will be perfect around the other side of the point. I think we'll pick up a ball over there rather than staying around here."

"Sounds like a good plan, but file it in the office. I've felt a few rumbles from our friend on the other side of the island." Presley jerked her thumb over her shoulder. It had been a while since the volcano had erupted. Everyone enjoyed it when she gave them downtime, but they walked around on tiptoe, waiting for her to spew ash and a little lava.

Kilauea could cause damage. She was a fucking volcano. But she was also a way of life for the people of Big Island.

"I'll listen for the reports." Jeff nodded. "But that cove is protected, and Kilauea generally pushes lava on the other side of the island. We won't be going there. Worst case if she erupts, I'll call for a dock at a marina."

"And stay with my boat." She lowered her chin. "Remember what happened with Fred's boat. Maritime law can be fucked up, but you abandon ship, and anyone can claim *Liberty*."

"You do love to quote the law." Jeff rolled his eyes. "And I can leave the boat once at port."

"You know what I was referring to." She squared her shoulders. But Jeff was partially right about her babbling on regarding different laws and procedures. Being a woman in this business was tough. She didn't sit behind the desk and crunch numbers. She ran the charters. She was a boat captain. And some people still haven't taken her seriously after all these years. She needed to not only show her skills, but state them as well.

Especially when Vernon still owned half.

Fucker.

"I got some bad news for you. Vernon's headed down the dock and he doesn't look happy." Adriana stood. "That's my cue to go back to my galley. That man scares me." She scurried through the doors.

"You're going to have to talk with him, boss. And you know why." Jeff squeezed her shoulder. "I'll be on the bow if you need me."

"Thanks." She tugged at her ponytail and stepped off the vessel and back onto the dock. This wasn't the first time her ex-husband had overbooked a charter. Every time he did this, it put her and her business in hot water. There were at least five bad reviews on the internet because of it and she was damn tired of Vernon's antics.

"What the fuck do you think you're doing?" Vernon marched closer, swaying his hands back and forth in that god-awful walk he had. "I just learned you tried to cancel my charter tomorrow. Thank God, I assured them that wasn't happening. You have to stop doing that. It's not good for business."

"I didn't try. I did cancel it." She folded her arms and widened her stance. She wasn't about to be bullied by Vernon. Not now. Not ever. He might still have a stake in her family business, but not for long. She would buy him out if it was the last thing she did.

Being tied to that man was going to be the death of her. Their marriage had been a union based on lies and manipulations. He was a swindler. A user. And nothing had changed.

Even three years after their divorce, he still had a choke hold over her life.

Motherfucker.

"You can't do that. I personally made the reservation. Frank Armstrong is a very important client of mine. I get his business, and it's smooth sailing for me. I need that charter to go out." Vernon planted his hands on his hips and glared. His nostrils flared in and out with each obnoxious breath. He practically foamed at the mouth like a damn rabid dog.

Client? That meant someone he wanted to swindle. Hawaii was filled with tourists. Rich tourists. Groups of people Vernon could use his charm to sweet-talk into investing in bullshit concepts and ideas that would never materialize.

When she first met him, he worked as a salesman for a time-share. He was so fucking good at it that Presley was in awe of him. Every sales job he touched, he succeeded.

Or so she thought.

"If you had gone through proper channels, you would have known that all the boats are booked."

"Um. I did look at the system." He cocked an arrogant brow. "I saw that *Waylen* wasn't in use." His lip twitched and his brow furrowed. "I can't believe you named a boat and then our fucking cat after an ex. That's cold, even for you."

"He was never your cat and blaming me for… We're not having this argument," she said. "I've asked you a million times to go through the proper channels when booking a charter."

Vernon laughed. "I own half this business, in case you've forgotten that detail. I walked into the office, looked at the schedule, and I saw what and who was available. It's not rocket science."

"If you had looked at the notes or hadn't bullied my staff, you would have seen that *Waylen* is scheduled for a tune-up." She lowered her chin. "She's not going out tomorrow, especially not for a five-day charter. I don't have a captain in the rotation that can go out for that long."

"Last I looked, you were a capable captain, and

you're who I scheduled." Vernon inched closer. "Look. Take this client out. Show him the kind of time that I know you can, because I've seen you in action. We might have had a shitty marriage, but I'm willing to give you kudos where they're deserved."

"Gee, thanks."

"You're welcome." He smiled. "Come on, Presley. We both need this. They are paying full fare. No discounts this time. I swear. They will tip well, that I can guarantee."

"It's a safety issue," she said.

"It's a newer boat. Waiting a week to get the engines serviced will not hurt."

"Not the point, and you know it."

"Do this and I'll consider selling you the rest of Driftwood Tours for half the market value."

"Don't fuck with me, Vernon. I don't have the time for this," she said. "Besides, I was planning on buying you out at the end of the season."

"We both know that's not going to happen. Your parents let this place get run-down and you've been scraping by ever since." He took her chin with his thumb and forefinger. "You make this charter work, or I will come in the same capacity as when we were married, and I will start making some changes around here. I'm tired of this business being barely profitable. We could be doing so many other things if you would listen to me. You know I'm good at what I do."

She didn't want him anywhere near this business. When he had full access, he'd fucked it all up. She'd made a deal with the devil and was now paying the price. Fucking hell. She should have known he was too good to be true when he came waltzing into Driftwood Tours with his dazzling smile and promises of making her life perfect and easy.

There was no such thing.

Her father always told her, *never trust a guy who says he has all the answers—except for Waylen.*

She bit back a smile.

Waylen had always been smarter than anyone she'd ever met. Her dad adored Waylen. Thought he was going places. That if anyone could make something out of nothing, it was Waylen. He wasn't a liar, and if he didn't have an answer, he wasn't too proud to admit it. But he'd immediately go looking for it.

"I want it in writing that you're going to give me half the market value," she said.

"If I land this deal, I will." He turned on his heel and strolled down the dock like he didn't have a care in the world.

She fisted her hands. "Ugh." She wanted to stomp her feet and scream at the top of her lungs like a damn toddler.

Or better yet, push the jerk into the ocean. He never liked swimming, especially in salt water. Who lived in Hawaii and didn't enjoy the perks of the lifestyle?

"Anyone ever tell you your ex-husband's a dick?" the sound of Blake's voice smacked her eardrums like a favorite song.

"Yeah, you every time you see him." Presley smiled as she approached one of the few women she called friend.

Presley had lived on Big Island her entire life. She'd grown up in this very marina. She'd never moved away, except for when she went to college. There were times in her life she had dreamed about leaving, but those fantasies were tied up with Waylen.

When she'd first met Waylen, he didn't believe he wanted to live anywhere else. But as they both got a little older, and he had visions of following in his father's footsteps, they would pull out the world map and stick pins in all the places they wanted to either visit or live.

Last she heard from Waylen, he'd gone to the Naval Academy, just like he'd always planned.

Good for him. She was proud that he'd done exactly what his dream had always been and what his father would have wanted. She assumed he'd had a career filled with travel, danger, and excitement.

All the things that made that man's heart sing.

"What did you see in that jerk?" Blake asked.

"Believe it or not, he was good in bed," Presley muttered. "Only place he wasn't a selfish prick."

"I still can't believe you and he ever did the dirty." Blake shook her head. "No offense. He's good-looking but seriously."

"Can we stop talking about him? It's depressing as hell."

"On one condition," Blake said. "We get a beer and you explain to me what you saw in Vernon and how you managed to stay married to him for seven years," Blake said.

"That isn't closing the topic." Presley laughed. "Make it tequila and I might consider having that conversation."

"That bad?"

"The fucking worst." Presley looped her arm through Blake's. They hadn't known each other long and Blake wasn't the kind of chick who required watering, so to speak. She was cool, easy, and laid-back.

Much like Presley wanted to be but couldn't. Her life had become too complicated, thanks to a few bad choices.

Her friendship with Blake didn't require too much nurturing. When they saw each other, they hung out. When they didn't, they didn't go out of their way or get their panties in a wad. Days or weeks could go by and they wouldn't see, hear, or text one another.

But if Blake needed Presley, or vice versa, they'd each come running.

That was the only kind of person Presley needed in her life these days. She didn't have the bandwidth to deal with any drama, and Blake certainly didn't bring that.

However, Blake had made it clear that she didn't like photos taken of herself, and she sure as shit didn't want images posted on social media. The only reason that had been brought up was because Presley used social media to promote her business and once asked Blake if she'd pose in front of one of her boats.

The answer was a big fat no followed by a please don't ever post a picture of her and no other reason was given.

Presley didn't press, but she had some suspicions. Whatever the reason, it didn't matter. Blake was good people.

"In one sentence, tell me what made you fall in love with a man like Vernon," Blake said.

"That's actually easy. In the beginning he was kind. Sweet. Other than having ideas, he didn't want to insert himself into my parents' business. But when my mom got sick, everything changed."

"How?"

"I was so wrapped up in helping my dad with

the business that Vernon got pissed. He wanted me to be at my mom's side. I thought that was so incredibly sensitive. He started taking a more serious interest in the business. He stepped up to the plate, but next thing I knew, my dad was freaking out."

"Over what?" Blake asked.

"All the stupid, crazy, fucked-up decisions Vernon was making, without even consulting either me or my dad. I swear to God that's what gave my father a heart attack and it was the beginning of the end of my marriage."

"Not that it's any of my business, but is Vernon making any money these days with his businesses?"

"He's up and down," Presley said. "I hate to admit it, but he does have some talents. The biggest one is to snow people. My dad warned me about not having a prenup. He really wanted me to push that with Vernon when we got married. I should have listened, but I didn't expect my father to die so suddenly, leaving me with something of value." She pursed her lips. "I couldn't say anything to my dad because I didn't want him to know that things in my marriage were that bad. He was so sad about my mom's passing. If I told him about what was happening with me and Vernon, it would have made things worse. All he ever wanted was to give me this business. He thought he was doing right by his little girl."

Blake shook her head. "You were stuck between a rock and a hard place."

"It sucked and as soon as my dad died, Vernon wanted to make all sorts of changes. But by then, I had finally grew a pair and my dad had his will set up so that I technically owned fifty-four percent. My dad at least did that right. However, when I divorced Vernon, he wouldn't give up his half and I still can't afford to buy him out."

"What did he want today?" Blake asked.

"He chartered a boat for a fucking five-day cruise—with me as captain of all things—for some asshole he's brownnosing about something."

"Why don't you tell him to fuck off?"

"Trust me, I did. But he's offering to let me buy him out for half the market value if I do this one thing for him."

"And you believe him?" Blake pushed open the door to the small marina bar. It was more like a skanky biker bar, but hey, it had beer, whiskey, and good tacos. What more did one need? Besides, it was owned by two of the best people in the area. She'd known Lisa and Al since she'd been in diapers.

"Not really, but if there's a chance he'll keep his word, I need to do it."

"I can't fault your logic there," Blake said. "First round's on me."

"You won't hear me argue." Presley climbed up

onto the stool. "So, what do you have going on this week?"

"Not much. A few local runs. One later in the week with the Brotherhood Protectors ranch. Other than that, same old shit, different day."

Presley set her cell on the counter and ordered her drink.

"I've never noticed this before, but is that a picture of you behind the bar?" Blake pointed.

"Yeah. That's me."

"Oh my God. You're adorable. How old were you?"

"I think thirteen."

"Who's the hottie?"

"Just some kid who used to hang around the marina. He and his dad had a boat here. They came fishing every chance they got. His dad was in the Navy. Deployed a lot, but fishing was their thing." Anytime anyone asked her what that boy's name was, she shrugged and told them it was a long time ago, avoiding saying his name out loud.

There were a handful of people who knew exactly who that boy was, but no one who knew her dared to mention his name, at least never to her. They knew better.

She only wished Al and Lisa would take down the damn thing.

"Is that picture over there him and his dad?"

"Yup." Presley really didn't want to get into this

conversation. She'd almost rather continue talking about Vernon.

"An old boyfriend?" Blake asked.

"Nope. Just a friend. He moved away a long time ago. I have no idea what happened to him." She stared into Waylen's eyes. He'd been fourteen in that picture. He'd just started his growth spurt and stood tall at five foot ten, but had yet to fill out. For a geek, he was incredibly handsome. He loved fishing and surfing. He also had a passion for reading and all things computers and video games. Waylen was the perfect human. He was kind, considerate, passionate, a daredevil, and the sweetest human she'd ever met. And she missed him with her whole heart.

For years, she'd chosen to forget about him. To push him out of her mind. Or at least she tried.

But the reality was, he was all she could ever think about.

"Here's to old and new friends." Blake raised her glass.

Presley smiled. Meeting Blake had been a godsend. The divorce had pushed Presley deep inside herself and further away from being social outside of those she worked with. She'd become untrusting, not just of others, but of her instincts and ability to read motivations and intentions of those around her, which made her crazy.

"To bitches in the air and in the sea. May we not crash and burn, nor sink," Presley said.

"That's the worst toast I've ever heard." Blake tapped her shot glass on the counter, tossed her head back, and downed the shot.

Presley did the same. She shivered. "Yeah, but it's a good thing to wish for, especially when I've got a boat going out that's ten hours past its service mark. That's never a good thing."

"You're meticulous with your boats. I'm sure it's fine."

Blake was right. Waylen was a solid vessel. Presley kept her boats in tip-top shape. She rarely let service go late and this boat hadn't had any issues since she'd bought it.

Presley was worrying for nothing.

Her fucking ex-husband had crawled under her skin. Nothing more. Nothing less.

2

*B*ig Island, Hawaii.

Of all the places Waylen Brown thought he'd end up for a retirement party for the best CO he'd ever had, this was not where he expected it to be.

Not that he was complaining.

Hawaii was the most beautiful place in the world.

However, it brought back a slew of memories and emotions that Waylen hadn't been prepared for.

He leaned against the fence, lifted his beer to his lips, and swigged. The barbecue was in full force. Jace "Hawk" Hawkins sure knew how to throw a party. Waylen knew it wouldn't be an intimate gathering. He'd done his best to prepare himself to be social, even though this kind of thing reminded him of when he'd been a teenager.

Hawk's ranch was an impressive piece of property that served as the base of operations for the local branch of the Brotherhood Protectors.

The men and women who worked for the organization were mainly retired from the military or ex-law enforcement.

It made Waylen think about what his future might look like now that he'd given civilian life a good run.

And it wasn't for him. He couldn't continue to travel with his buddies for the rest of his life. He wasn't interested in chasing women. His ex-wife had left such a bad taste in his mouth that he'd barely dated since then.

Going without a girl in his bed was easy.

However, living his life outside of the Navy had become a chore.

Military life might have run its course, but he wasn't an old man at forty. He needed to keep the blood pumping in his veins, and an organization like the Brotherhood Protectors might just be exactly what he and his team were looking for.

Though, they'd come to Big Island to celebrate a great man and Waylen wasn't sure his heart and soul could bear the pains of the past that Big Island and all of Hawaii represented.

"What the hell are you doing over here, all by your lonesome?" Harlan Fender strolled across the grass with that cool swagger that often made him appear a little arrogant and difficult to read.

Harlan was far from egotistical. He had this even keel about him that reminded Waylen of one of his favorite types of catamarans. The sailboat would cut through the water with a steady, sturdy, reliable hull.

That was Harlan.

But most regarded him as a standoffish personality type.

It wasn't true. But he could be guarded, which was a hazard of the job.

Harlan was a top-notch negotiator. He had to remain calm in all situations and that's precisely what he did—to a fucking fault. It sometimes drove Waylen nuts, but it was also one of the things that Waylen admired.

"Taking in the view." Waylen raised his long-neck and clanked it against Harlan's.

"How's it feel to be back?"

Waylen shrugged. This was not a conversation he wanted to have, except maybe with his mother. Not even with one of his closest friends. Too many demons. Too many memories of his dad. Or a certain girl whom he could never quite get out of his mind.

Or heart.

"Everything looks smaller than I remember. I sent my mom a bunch of pictures and she said it all looks a little different, but exactly the same. I have no idea what she means by that, but it made her cry." Waylen sighed. "I'm thinking about flying her out here in a couple of weeks."

"I'm sure she'd like that." Harlan nodded. "We've been in some pretty amazing places. But this is spectacular. It must have been incredible to grow up here."

"It was," Waylen said. "But Chesapeake Bay was nice too. Great fishing and all my aunts, uncles, and cousins are there."

But Presley wasn't.

He sighed. That name had been stuck in his head since he had landed, and he couldn't get it out.

"Your uncle Ricky cracks me up. He tries to out-negotiate me every time I see him."

Waylen laughed. "He thinks you're the bomb."

"Looks like you two are in deep conversation," Raider Torres said, jogging over. "Or are we looking for a one-night stand for Harlan?"

"I'm always on high alert for that." One thing Waylen could count on from Raider was comic relief. If you're going to be an explosives expert, you had to have a sense of humor to go with the insanity that went with that job. But Raider had not taken to civilian life as well as everyone else. No one had adjusted easily, but Waylen had taken to it the best. He'd been the most ready to retire from active duty.

It wasn't that Raider wasn't, but the lack of action had been fucking with his mental stability.

"You boys are real funny." Harlan took a swig of his brew. "What do you think of this place and of the Brotherhood Protectors?"

"Check and check," Raider said. "I'd consider both." That had been the most excitement Raider had shown about anything outside of a near-death experience since they had walked off the base.

"I know a guy who works for the Colorado branch." Waylen fiddled with the label on his beer. "We crossed paths while doing some IT training. His name is Darius Ford. He was Army. Worked a lot of JSOC missions. Great guy. You think I've got skills, that man's a fucking genius. He's got nothing but great things to say about this organization and everyone in it."

"That's good to know." Raider lifted his arm, resting his elbow on one of the posts. Raider was the kind of man you didn't want to fuck with, but he was also as loyal as they came. He was the type of man who, if you asked for help, didn't ask why, he just did. "Anyone seen Lane lately?"

Waylen chuckled. "When I left him, he was chatting up some cute little thing. Man is always flirting with someone."

"That's for damn sure," Harlan said. "I'm going to go get some grub. You two idiots coming?"

"In a couple." Waylen nodded. "I need to call my mom."

"You've always been a bit of a mama's boy," Raider said.

"And proud of it." Waylen blinked a few times and cracked a grin.

Harlan squeezed his shoulder. "Get your ass over to the food and stop being antisocial. It's not good for you."

"I'm with him on that," Raider said.

Waylen waved his cell. "I'll be there in ten." He tapped the icon where he stored the images from his past. A part of him had thought about looking Presley up, but it had been twenty-three years. For all he knew, she could be married with a bunch of kids.

Hell, he'd tried wedded bliss.

He chuckled. More like wedded hell. That marriage had only lasted five years.

"Hey, man."

Waylen glanced up.

Lane Benning practically skipped in his direction. Of all the men on the team, Lane could often be the most animated, which was funny. He was a sniper. He had to be calm. Quiet. Relaxed, but ready to fire.

Lane had a happy-go-lucky attitude about life. Not much rattled his nerves. He was like Harlan in that sense. But the difference between the two men was Lane didn't make everything a massive discussion.

"Did you get lucky?" Waylen asked.

"I might have gotten a phone number." Lane grinned. "She probably has a friend."

Waylen shook his head. "I can get my own dates, thank you very much."

"I'll believe that when I see it." Lane cocked his head. "They're serving food over there."

"Did you come all the way over here to tell me that, or are my teammates coming over one by one to check on me?" Everyone knew about his dad. It was no secret that his father had died from a widow-maker heart attack when Waylen was sixteen years old. Six months later, his mom packed up all their things and they moved from Big Island, Hawaii, where his father had been stationed, back to Maryland.

Waylen's hero had always been his dad. Losing him had been one of the toughest things he'd ever had to go through. SEAL training was easier than the first few months after his father's death.

And Waylen still carried that pain etched deep in his soul.

But he'd lost something else when he moved from Hawaii at the age of seventeen, and he'd never forgotten her.

"You can take care of yourself." Lane chuckled, but his face quickly turned serious as he ran a hand across his mouth. "Look. You and I go back a long time. We've seen some shit together. Surfed some gnarly waves." He placed his hand on Waylen's chest. "I know what you're going through. I know how hard it is for you to be back here, especially on this island. You were there for me when I scattered my mom's ashes." He arched a brow. "I'm here for you now. Whenever you're ready, all you have to do is ask." Lane had brought the whole team to Malibu when it came time to spread his dear sweet mother's ashes. They had surrounded him when he needed their support the most.

Waylen didn't know what he wanted. One minute, he wanted the team with him when he spread his father's ashes, the next, he wanted to go find Presley.

His teammates, every single one of them, teased him for being an introvert. A computer geek. That he'd rather spend a night home with his gadgets, instead of a warm body.

Have a marriage like his and you might prefer binge-watching a show than being with someone who can make your life a living horror show.

"I appreciate that and when the time comes, I'll let you know."

Lane nodded. "Now, let's go eat."

"I promised my mom I'd check in, so I need to call her." He lowered his chin and waved his cell.

"You're a good boy." Lane turned and meandered back toward the party.

Waylen tapped his mother's number and placed it on speaker. He glanced around the farm, his gaze landing on one of his oldest and best friends, Kian Fox.

He burst out laughing.

"What's so funny, son?" his mother's voice echoed into the evening air.

"I'm looking at Kian staring intently at a woman, drooling over her."

"Good. That man should have a nice lady in his life," his mom said. "So should you."

"Don't start, Ma. I tried that once. You remember how it ended."

"She was a class A bitch."

"Why don't you tell me how you really feel about my ex-wife." He chuckled.

"I wouldn't want to hurt your poor, sensitive ears," she said. "How's everything going in Hawaii? Aren't you supposed to be at the party for Glenn Gadsden?"

"I promised you I'd call." He was also avoiding all the people. No one could call Waylen shy. It wasn't that. He knew how to carry a conversation. But given the choice between being alone with nature and shooting the shit about the good old days, he'd take his quiet thoughts.

"I know it's hard for you to be back there. Especially Big Island. But you can't retreat inside your-self. You do that too much as it is."

"I promise you, I'm not. We found this great little bar that me and the boys went and hung out at once already. Lane and I went surfing. We're all having a great time. Really, Mom. Now I need to find the right place to take Dad. I thought I'd rent a boat and take him to one of our favorite fishing spots."

His mom let out that cute little giggle that made her sound so youthful. "No. You liked to go look at some cute brunette and used fishing as your excuse."

"That too." He raked his hand over the top of his head. "What do you think?"

"We always agreed to spread Daddy's ashes in Hawaii. I'm not there and you are. Do what feels right."

"I believe that does. It's not far from our old home, which I'm thinking about taking a trip over there too."

"Oh, Waylen. I'd love to see pictures of that."

"I was thinking you should come out. I could book you a ticket."

"No," his mother said quickly. Too quickly. It was her standard response and she never changed her mind. "You know how I feel about going back."

"It might do you some good." He let out a long breath. Since his dad had died, his mom had chosen to live her life alone. His father had been the love of her life and she didn't want to date. Waylen respected that. His mom got out of the house. She had friends. She had a life.

But there was always a sadness.

"I'd love to share some of this trip with you. Will you at least think about it? For me?"

"Oh, that's not fair to do to your mother," she muttered. "It's that important to you?"

"It is," he admitted.

"All right. I'll think about it."

"How about next week?"

"I've got your cousin's baby shower that I'm hosting."

"Fine, the week after. I'll book the flight."

"You're not going to let me say no, are you?"

"Ma, I think this will be good for both of us."

"All right," she said. Is there anything else? I don't want you to use this phone call as an excuse for not socializing. You do tend to do that a lot, and while I love hearing your voice, I want you to enjoy the party and your time there."

"I do have a burning question for you," he said.

"And what, dare I ask, is that?"

"It's the ring. Why was it so important to you that I bring your engagement ring with me? I know I screwed up by giving it to Elena. I should have listened when you told me you didn't want her to have it. The ring is tainted now."

"Just because that crazy woman wore it, that doesn't make the ring cursed. Your father gave it to me and we had a wonderful marriage. So stop saying stupid shit. Most of our good years were on Big Island. We raised you there. Our best memories are there. I thought it would give you comfort."

"That's so weird considering I had such a shitty relationship with Elena and how you feel about her."

"Maybe, but you never spent any time there with your ex-wife. That ring isn't about your marriage, but about me and your father. About our family. It was always meant to stay with family. For a brief time, Elena was family and we can't change the past. That ring is meant to be with you. You'll figure it out. Now, go be social. Enjoy yourself. Stop standing off to the side. Get out of your head for once in your life."

"Yes, Mother." He chuckled. He did not know what she meant, but he'd do anything for his mom. She was his rock. His foundation. People could call him a mama's boy all they wanted, he didn't give a shit. He wore that title proudly. "I love you. I'll call you in a day or two."

"I love you too, son."

He ended the call, polished off the rest of his beer, squared his shoulders, and headed toward the lights, music, and all the people.

God, he hated crowds. When he'd been a

teenager, his old man teased him that Waylen only liked three things.

Fishing.

Surfing.

And gadgets.

That wasn't entirely false.

Waylen had always been more comfortable with computers rather than people. In first grade, his teachers realized he not only surpassed his classmates in reading, but his math skills were already at a third-grade level. At that age, being taken out of class for special treatment seemed like a treat. But in the end, it alienated him from kids his own age. Being a little genius didn't do him any favors until it was time to go to the Naval Academy.

In middle and high school, he didn't have many friends. If he hadn't been bigger than half the class, and graced with muscles at an early age, he might have been picked on more. But that still didn't help with his social life. Being labeled a nerd had been the kiss of death.

Except with Presley.

He pushed her out of his thoughts. They'd been kids. She'd gone on to have a life and possibly gotten off this island.

Driftwood Tours.

Her parents' business.

It was nothing short of a miracle that he hadn't even googled the business yet. But part of him didn't want to know if she had anything to do with it because, deep down, he figured she did.

"Kian," Waylen said, though he kept his voice soft because he could. Teasing his buddy was about one of the best pastimes outside of playing video games.

Nothing.

"Yo. Kian."

The man didn't move. Just stared at the pretty lady in front of the chopper.

Waylen nudged his shoulder.

Kian whipped his head around, nearly socking Waylen in the chest. Kian wiped his hand across his mouth. "Jesus, buddy. Don't sneak up on me like that."

"I didn't sneak up on you. I walked across the grass." Waylen laughed.

"Well, next time, make more noise because the band's got it cranked so high that the ground's vibrating."

"It's not that loud. And I called your name." Waylen leaned closer for effect. "Twice." He chose to leave out the fact that he'd barely whispered the man's name.

Kian shrugged. "I guess I got distracted admiring what Hawk's got going on here."

Waylen arched a brow, nodding at the helipad. "Can't argue with you there. She's a beauty. Is that a gardenia on her ass?"

Kian snapped his gaze back to the chopper.

Jesus, this was too easy and too much fucking fun.

"As a matter of fact, it is," Kian said.

"Maybe the pilot has one tattooed on her backside too, because it was her ass you were staring at, right?"

"Well, it sure as hell wasn't yours. You done being antisocial, or are you just taking a break so you can bust my balls?"

Waylen flipped him off. "I don't need a reason to do that. Besides, you know I don't like crowds." Waylen arched his back. He glanced around. There was no place in the world like Hawaii and it truly was like coming home.

"And I don't like volcanoes, yet here I am, standing beside Hawaii's most active one."

"It's a good thirty miles away. Hardly right next door."

"Still…" Kian leaned against the bar, taking another swig. "So, what do you think about Hawk and his setup? Lane says the others are antsy to get back into the fray."

Waylen shrugged, although the conflicting emotions made him pause. On the one hand, working for an outfit like the Brotherhood Protectors would be a match made in heaven.

Doing it in Hawaii might be too close to all those personal demons he'd been trying to keep at bay. "It's definitely got potential. I know someone who works for the Colorado branch and he's got nothing but great things to say about the Brotherhood and the CEO, Hank Patterson."

Kian gave Waylen the side-eye. "Is that a yes if you were given the chance to join?"

"Maybe. I…" Waylen took another look around the party, scanning the people. Familiar faces. Strangers. Families. This had been home for so many years. When he'd first left, he'd longed to return. The first year at the Naval Academy, he'd wondered what it would have been like if he'd made different choices. If he'd defied his mother—and his dream—and returned to Big Island. However, by the middle of the second year, he was all in, and while Hawaii and all that it represented was still glued to his soul, he did his best to move on. "I guess I just never considered coming back here to stay."

Kian nudged his shoulder. "Which brings up my next point… Are you okay? Because you've been noticeably distant since—"

The bottom of his feet rumbled.

He remembered that sensation and it wasn't a good feeling.

Kilauea.

Waylen braced for what could be a small disruption. Or a massive one. He glanced toward the sky.

First came the white and gray smoke.

Then the ash.

Red mixed with black filled the sky and then dumped in the direction of the ocean.

The ground under Waylen's feet rattled much like a minor earthquake. The party had come to a standstill.

The sun disappeared behind what appeared to clouds, but that was an illusion.

"And there goes the volcano, which means you owe me fifty bucks," Kian said.

"For what?" Waylen glared.

"You promised me this would be a lava-free vacation, remember? Said, and I quote, 'Kilauea's sleeping. You'll be fine.'"

"You are fine, jackass, and I can't help if the damn volcano decides to erupt."

"A bet's a bet."

Waylen mumbled a few cuss words under his breath as he reached for his wallet, handing Kian a fifty-dollar bill. "No one likes a sore winner, buddy."

Kian grinned, shoving the money in his pocket. "Don't get mad at me because you chose poorly. You should know better than to bet on something you can't control."

"I read the reports. She wasn't supposed to erupt anytime soon. Though, this new development does complicate things. I think we should go find the others," Waylen said with his blood pumping like a raging wildfire. It had been a long time since he'd been called to action, and he wasn't about to sit back when his skills could be put to good use.

Not even in Hawaii.

Especially not on Big Island.

A place he once called home and bloody hell, it still felt that way.

3

*P*resley sat behind the helm and studied the radar. Two systems had appeared out of nowhere. It wasn't uncommon for that to happen out in the ocean. But when the wind kicked up to twenty knots and shifted directions, that was the moment that gave Presley pause.

It got worse when Kilauea sputtered and spewed to life fifteen minutes ago.

"Do we need to be worried about that volcano?" Frank asked, sticking his head up the ladder. "And it's pretty rough. We're all feeling a little seasick."

She could only go so fast in swells four to six feet. It wasn't a good day at sea.

"I'm sorry about the rolls. Not much I can do but get us to the next cove as safely as possible." She pointed. "It's going to be a bit. We can't pick up a buoy where I had originally planned because to be honest, I don't know what Kilauea has in store for us. I've radioed ahead to a marina not far from here. We've got a slip and that's where I'm headed."

"It looks like we're driving toward danger, not away from it," Frank said.

"I know it looks that way. But I need to get us to the nearest marina. Unfortunately, that means a little rougher ride with these swells. We're about five miles from shore. The closer we get, the better it will be."

"Any chance we can make some grilled cheese sandwiches or something? Food always calms my stomach."

"Feel free to talk with the chef. He can help you out in that department." A big meal was out of the question, but if she could keep Frank, his wife, and their friends occupied in the cabin and out of her way while she navigated toward shore and the marina where she could pick up dock space, all the better.

Thank God, the wind was pushing them toward shore, not away, giving her wind speed since she couldn't knock up the engine speed in these swells.

"Thanks." Frank ducked his head into the galley.

She studied the instruments. The interval between the swells was only five seconds. Add in the wind gusts, and it made for a nasty ride. This was not the kind of weather she liked to be stuck in.

When she radioed into the marina, they warned her that if the winds shifted, ash and lava could be pushed in their direction.

But she needed to get out of the open ocean and picking up a buoy around the corner in front of the volcano wasn't an option.

A big whooshing noise echoed from down below, followed by a deafening noise.

The boat pitched to the port side.

Screams echoed from below.

Presley gripped the helm as her body was flung into the side rail of the captain's perch. Curling her fingers over the throttles, she pulled them to neutral, but it turned out to be unnecessary because both engines cut out.

The fire alarm rang. Followed by a different alarm.

The catamaran bounced in the water like a toy in a bathtub.

Fire and smoke billowed out of the galley.

Remi, her deckhand, stood in the center with a fire extinguisher. His clothes were scorched and burn marks lined his arms.

"I need help." Harry was on the floor with Frank. "The stove blew up and he's badly hurt." Harry glanced up.

"Oh my God!" Frank's wife was on her knees.

Frank moaned and groaned.

"Frank. Talk to me," Melissa said. "Honey. Oh no, he's unconscious now."

A spark illuminated off the control panel.

Quickly, she raced to it and shut off the breaker that controlled the gas lines.

Another spark.

The batteries went dead.

She jerked back. "Shit." An eerie silence filled the air. "Make sure that fire is completely out."

"Yes, ma'am," Remi said. "It was the gas line. As soon as the customer turned on the stove, it went up. It's the only thing that makes sense."

"Ma'am." She touched Melissa's shoulders. "I know you're scared and concerned. We're all trained for this. I need you and the rest of the guests to sit at the table on the aft deck. Remi will tend to your husband. Is there anything he's allergic to or does he have any medical conditions we need to know about?" In all her life, this was by far the worst situation she'd ever been in at sea, and she'd seen shit. Her heart raced.

Melissa shook her head. "I'm not leaving his side."

"All right. But please do exactly what Remi says. He's certified in first aid." She swallowed as she took in the wounds consisting of massive burns on his face and upper body.

Frank blinked open his eyes. His lips parted, but only a grumble echoed from his mouth.

"Don't try to talk," Remi said. "Stay still."

"Everyone to the stern table." Presley pointed.

"We're lucky it wasn't worse." Remi set the fire extinguisher to the side. "One of the other guests acted quickly when they saw the spark and shut the pilot off." He got to his knees and opened the first aid kit. "I've got a good pulse. But it's the burns and the fact he's in and out of consciousness that concerns me."

Presley squeezed Melissa's shoulder. "I'm going to do a quick assessment of the boat and radio for help. It's going to be okay."

She fiddled with the instruments. They weren't pulling any more power than any other charter. There was plenty of juice. It didn't make sense.

"Without gas, we can't fire up the generator, which would give us power." Remi ran a hand through his shoulder-length hair. He was a native of the islands and had gone to school with Presley. After graduation, he'd moved away to the mainland. He'd wanted to be an actor and a model. He'd managed some success. But after his wife left him for a younger man, he returned to Hawaii for what he described as a life of serenity.

Now, he had a wife and a two-year-old daughter. He was about as happy and serene as they came.

"What can we do?" one of the other guests asked.

"Put on these life jackets. Just as a precaution."

Presley lifted the hatch where the majority of the vests were and began handing them out just as another set of alarms went off.

Fucking bilge pumps.

"Harry, stay with the guests and help Remi." Presley rubbed the back of her neck. A million checklists rattled through her brain. But mostly, she repeated the mantra, *stay calm*, over and over again as the waves kicked up, lifting the boat, rocking it port and starboard and bow to stern.

If anyone was going to be seasick, now was going to be the time.

"Sure thing." Harry gave her a weak smile.

She went to the port, center bilge, lifting the hatch. "Goddammit," she muttered. She climbed the three steps to the captain's chair and snagged the mic. "Mayday! Mayday! Mayday! This is *Waylen*, *Waylen*, *Waylen*. Call number Bravo Vector, nine, eight, two, four, six, seven. Mayday! This is *Waylen*. I've got an injured passenger who needs to go to the hospital and I'm dead in the water."

Remi came up behind her and placed his hand on her shoulder. "It's a little rough to go this route, but we do have the tender."

"I'm not abandoning ship." She glared.

"I can't send Henry with the guests. He's not qualified. And I'm not leaving you here alone," Remi said. "The seas are getting worse. The volcano is officially active. The safest thing to do is—"

"You know what happens if a captain leaves his vessel. I'm not losing this boat." She lifted the mic. "If it comes to someone saying we need to motor in the tender to get help, you can go. But I'm not leaving."

"You're the captain."

She blew out a puff of air and glanced toward the angry sky. "Come on, Daddy. If I ever needed your guidance from heaven, today would be the day."

Waylen climbed into the back of a helicopter operated by a woman named Blake Garrett. He did his best to keep his smirk to himself. Only the second the pretty lady his buddy was crushing hard on had her back to them did he let loose with the grin.

Fuck off, Kian mouthed.

"Not going to happen," he yelled over the engine's roar. The rattle of the bird's metal got his adrenaline going. The good old days. He missed the action, but not the military. It was an odd sensation.

"You two buckled in back there?" she called over the mic.

"Ready to roll," Kian said before moving the

comms out of the way. "I wish I felt as relaxed as you look." He tugged at the harness. "I can't say I'm thrilled about flying through the thick ash and smoke of a fucking volcano."

Waylen shrugged. Thanks to Kilauea and her rumblings, he'd been evacuated from his home at least half a dozen times as a teenager. His old man had taken him up twice in a buddy's chopper during one of her more aggressive eruptions. It was exhilarating as much as it was terrifying. "We'll be fine."

"And you know this how?"

Waylen laughed. "The same way I knew we would get out alive during Operation Hamster."

"Jesus, that was a fucked-up mission and you got shot. I had to drag your ass out over my shoulder. How can you be so cavalier about this entire situation?" He jerked his head toward the pilot. "And with a stranger?"

"Miss Gardenia? Come on. Are you telling me when she drops us off back at the ranch, you won't ask her for her number?"

"That's a different conversation," Kian said, adjusting his straps for the second time as the chopper lifted from the ground with a jerk. "And I'm not sure it's a good idea to call her that."

Waylen looked out the window. Volcanoes were a way of life on the islands, much like surfing and sharks. There wasn't much anyone could do to stop Kilauea's wrath, just like sharks swam in the ocean.

But he wasn't a fool. Circling a volcano wasn't for the faint of heart. He understood it was a necessary evil in understanding which towns might already be at risk and who needed to be evacuated early.

The bird hovered for a moment before pitching forward as it gained altitude. A million memories bombarded Waylen's mind again.

Flying with his father and his friends.

Boating with his dad, Presley, and her father.

They blended in a mirage of happiness and emptiness.

He missed his dad in the worst way. His old man had been his champion. His best friend.

And Presley... Jesus. He needed to get her out of his mind. It was fucking stupid.

"Hey, man." Kian tapped Waylen's knee. "What's going on with you?" Kian arched a brow. "And don't give me the song and dance about your dad." He held up his hand. "I'm not belittling the emotions you must be feeling, but I know you. It's more than that, so why don't you tell me what's going on before we plummet to our death circling this volcano."

"That's a bit dramatic." Waylen shifted, collecting his thoughts. If there was anyone he'd trust with this, it would be Kian. "But you're right. We're gonna die."

"You're a dick." Kian nudged his leg. "Now spill what has you so fucking melancholy I want to jump from this chopper right into the center of that damn spewing fireball."

The helicopter banked right.

A flash from the volcano lit up the sky.

Waylen tightened his harness. It was going to be a bumpy ride. "You remember how my ex-wife took issue with all the things I wanted to keep of my dad's and from my time here in Hawaii?"

"Elena was a bitch." Kian shook his head. "Sorry, man. I know she was your wife, but I couldn't stand her even when you first married her."

"Yeah, well, I'm not sure what I saw in her either." That wasn't an entirely true statement. Elena did have some good qualities, especially early on. She could be kind. She had a big heart. She volunteered at the local animal shelter. He loved that about her, but she could also be insanely selfish and self-centered. If the world wasn't revolving around her, she made sure people stopped and paid attention to whatever she was doing.

And she had to be in control.

Of everything.

It drove his mother and the rest of his family nuts. Elena came in like a wrecking ball if they were having a family gathering. Things had to be done her way, even when it wasn't at their house.

"It wasn't just my dad's stuff she took issue with me keeping," Waylen said.

45

"I remember she threatened to toss your old surfboard into the fire."

"That was never going to happen." Waylen chuckled. "Anyway. I kept a small box from high school. It had a few pictures and handwritten notes that pissed her off."

Kian jerked his head back. "Pictures of a girl? Love notes from a chick? From when you were a teenager. You kept that shit?"

"Something like that," Waylen said.

"You were seventeen when you left this island. Just a stupid kid. Are you trying to tell me that a young girl had ahold of you so bad you couldn't let her go? And I'm just hearing about it now."

"Presley wasn't just any girl. She's the first one I've ever loved. Maybe the only one I ever truly loved." Damn, what a weird thing to admit out loud. Even to Kian. "After my dad died, I knew my mom was thinking about moving back to Maryland, but I thought she'd wait until after I finished high school. Instead, she moved us off the island before the start of my senior year. She didn't even give me a chance to process. She told me on a Monday. We were gone that Friday. No amount of begging on my part—or even Presley's—helped."

"Don't hit me, but you were headed for the Naval Academy and Maryland anyway. What difference did it make?"

Waylen shrugged. "I don't know. Before my dad

died, there was a part of me that wasn't sure I wanted to go. I talked about going to college in Hawaii. Staying with Presley. My mom thought I was nuts. Oddly, my dad and I had some pretty amazing conversations about it."

"You told me your father always wanted you to join the Navy."

"He encouraged it," Waylen said. "And he made it clear that no matter what, I wasn't to piss away all the insane talents I was given. I was going to college. But he wasn't going to force the Academy on me, even if we had already started the process."

"I can't imagine life without you having gone there or being in the Navy."

Waylen smiled. "I honestly can't either and Presley wanted me to do it. She and I argued more about whether or not I should enlist more than my parents and I did. But to be fair, me joining was a lifelong dream. And not just because of my dad. I was a nerd growing up. I got picked on relentlessly. Part of me needed to prove to myself and those assholes I could sit at the badass table."

"You're still a fucking geek. You might be able to kick my ass, but that doesn't take away your *king of the nerds* title. However, what does any of this have to do with the fact you're carrying a torch for a girl you knew over twenty years ago?"

Waylen glanced out the window. "It's strange. I tried to forget Big Island and everything about this place when I went to the Naval Academy. I packed up everything I'd kept and put the boxes in my mom's basement. I didn't throw them away because my mother suggested that I give myself space and time. That if, when I came home, I still wanted to purge the memories, then four years later would be the time."

"But you never did."

Waylen shifted his gaze and shrugged. "Both the box and girl became out of sight, out of mind."

"Then how did Elena come to find the pictures and love notes?"

"When my mom moved from the big house on the bay to the townhouse, she made me take all the crap I'd left behind. I got rid of some of it, but not those things from Presley. I brought them home and put them in my closet." He raised his hand. "This was before I married Elena. However, she wasn't happy when she found them, and even more pissed off that I wouldn't let her toss them away."

"I can't believe I'm going to say this, but I don't blame the woman."

"You're going to take her side? Really? I thought you were my best friend!"

Kian poked the center of his chest. "Best buds tell each other everything and you kept this Presley woman from me for a very long fucking time."

"Jealousy is not a good look on you, man." Waylen shook his head. "Don't you have someone in your past that tugs at your heartstrings every once in a while? Or does Miss Gardenia up there have your panties in such a twist it's cutting off the circulation to your brain?"

"Look who's being an asshole now." Kian lowered his chin. "So, tell me. What makes this Presley chick so special?"

"It's hard to put into—"

A crackle came over the radio.

"Everything's fine, but there's a change in plans," Blake said.

"What kind of change?" Kian asked with wide eyes.

"Before I go into any details, I need to know what you boys did in the service. And I'm really hoping it involved rescue swimming; otherwise, this is going to be very awkward."

Waylen glanced at Kian and smiled.

"We're SEALs, so I think we've got a bit of experience under our belts," Kian said.

"Finally, a surprise I can get behind. I just received a mayday call from a vessel that's dead in the water with at least one injured passenger on board who'll require airlifting to the nearest hospital. We're five minutes out. I will need one of you in the water and the other to stay with me to man the hoist. I've got a rescue ladder and a collapsible basket on the middle front seat."

The bird banked right and pitched down.

Jesus, the woman flew like she'd been in the military herself.

Kian reached over and unbuckled Waylen's harness.

"What the fuck are you doing?" Waylen glared. "I'm not jumping."

"The hell you aren't."

"I believe I did this the last time you and I were in the back of a chopper together."

"I've got the boat in my sights. Once one of you is on board, switch to channel twenty-four so we can communicate," Blake said over the comms. "You can open the doors now. The wind's going to really kick us around, especially once you're hanging below. It'll be easier to jump using the ladder. Whoever's staying with me can let me know when your partner's fifteen feet off the water so I can hold her steady, but this isn't going to be pretty. Get ready, and whatever you do, don't drown."

"Consider this payback for not telling me about this woman you've been pining over for twenty-three years." Kian gripped his shirt and grinned.

"You're a fucking asshole, you know that?" Waylen let out a long breath, glancing over his shoulder as the bird hovered over the angry ocean, inching closer.

The mast of the catamaran danced like a wild drunken sailor.

Waylen gripped the sides of the bird while Kian

kicked the ladder out the door. Waylen shimmied down it until he was at the last rung. He glanced up, gave the thumbs-up, and released, bracing himself for impact.

He'd done this a million times. To him, it was part of the job.

But it still fucking hurt the second his feet hit the water.

And this was no exception.

Add in the rough seas, and reentry was going to be a bitch.

Splash!

He held his breath, letting his body relax. The key was not to panic. He waited a couple of seconds before charging to the surface. Once he broke, he looked left and right until he found the boat.

Waylen.

What the fuck.

Driftwood Tours.

Jesus. It couldn't be.

He swam toward the stern with his heart firmly planted in his throat.

A woman's silhouette lowered the attached metal ladder into the water and stretched out her hand.

Her long dark hair was pulled back into a ponytail.

He locked gazes with those hauntingly familiar blue eyes as he reached for her hand.

His foot slipped on the first rung of the ladder.

"Presley?" He hoisted himself onto the boat and ran his fingers through his wet hair. She didn't look that much different. A few wrinkles around the eyes that came with age. There was a maturity that wasn't there when he'd left, but again, years of living. "You named your boat after me?"

"That's what you're going to lead with after all these years?" She looked him up and down. "I can't believe you're standing on my boat."

"A million things are going through my brain right now, but Miss Gardenia mentioned an injured passenger."

"Gardenia? Who the fuck is that?"

He chuckled. Her foul mouth hadn't changed. Nor had her stunning figure. Her captivating eyes. Or her beauty.

But he had a job to do.

"Blake. The helicopter pilot."

"Can't imagine where or why you'd give her that name, but don't ever let her hear you call her that. I doubt she'd appreciate it." Presley curled her fingers around his biceps and gave him a good yank.

Still as strong as ever.

"We must have had a gas leak. It blew the pilot on the stove. I've got a passenger slipping in and out of consciousness with some nasty burns on his face and torso. I need to get him to a hospital and transport all the passengers and my crew to shore."

"And what about you?"

"Coast Guard is thirty minutes out." She planted her hands on her hips. "I'm not abandoning ship."

"Are you taking on water?"

"Not the point." She arched a brow.

"Jesus, Presley." He sucked in a deep breath. She'd always been a stubborn human. And loved her maritime laws. "You're sending everyone off with the tender and you plan on staying on a boat that's dead in the water while it's sinking."

"I'm the captain of this vessel. You, of all people, should understand what that means when it comes to—"

"Don't go quoting maritime law to me." He'd have this argument with her later.

He glanced at the mast. "That bird can't hover over this cat for me to lift him onto the ladder."

"What about the tender? I know it's rough out there, but you can get a safe distance from the mast."

He made his way to the helm and fiddled with the dial. "Blake, this is Waylen, do you read?"

"Copy," Blake said.

"We're doing this the hard way," he said. "I'm loading the injured passenger in a tender. I'll go fifty feet from the stern." He shifted his gaze. "While I'm prepping the injured, I need you to radio the puddle pirates—I mean the Coast Guard. Presley says

53

they're thirty minutes out. But she's taking on water. We need them sooner."

"Tell her I said to abandon—"

"Already told her and I'll be repeating it. For now, let's deal with one situation at a time. The tender has no lights. All you'll see is a headlamp." He turned, locking gazes with Presley. "You do have one of those, right?"

"Don't be a dick. It's not a good look for you." She cocked her head and pursed her lips. It was the same look she'd given him the day they got stranded on the reef. It hadn't been her fault, but his. However, it was her family's boat and he decided to be an ass and ask her stupid questions about whether or not she had proper safety equipment.

Which she had.

Because Presley was a stickler for that shit.

He stepped into the galley and was horrified by the sight. She was damn lucky the entire boat wasn't at the bottom of the ocean. A hole had been blown out the side of the galley above the stove. It wasn't a big one, but the damage had been done.

The guest in question lay sprawled out on the floor and he wasn't looking pretty.

"Melissa," Presley said softly. "This is Waylen. He's an old friend of mine and he went to the Naval Academy. In that helicopter up there is another good friend. They're going to get you and your husband to a hospital."

"Ma'am." Waylen knelt next to the woman. "I'm a retired SEAL. I did this kind of thing all the time. My buddy, Kian, is up in the chopper. He's a combat medic. Your husband is in good hands."

"Thank you." Melissa swiped at her cheeks.

"Tender's ready." Remi held the tender steady. "Man, it's wild to see you again."

"You too." Waylen nodded. Remi had been one of the few people in high school who hadn't busted his balls for being such a nerd.

Gently, Waylen lifted the injured man and carried him to the stern. He laid him on the floor of the tender. "Remi, I'm going to need you to come with me."

"I've got your back. Just like old times." Remi crawled to the back of the tender.

Waylen released the line. "Go."

The tender jerked back, then forward, heading toward the chopper.

He adjusted the headlamp.

The water spread out as the wind swirled. The helicopter approached and lowered the basket closer. He waved his hand once over his head at Kian as he reached for the basket.

He missed the first time.

He snagged it the second time. As quickly as he could, he loaded the passenger into the basket. He gave the whirlybird sign to Kian and released the basket.

The ladder slowly rose toward the chopper as it moved away from the tender and catamaran.

"Let's get this tender back to the boat so you can get the rest of the passengers to shore." Waylen raked his fingers through his wet hair. His pounding pulse matched the whopping of the blades. He stared at the boat in the dark water.

No lights.

No power.

Two miles from shore.

The wind shifted, pushing them in the right direction. That helped.

However, the gravity of the situation smacked him between the eyes. He knew there was no way he was going to get Presley to leave that damn boat.

Named fucking *Waylen.*

At least she'd never forgotten him; that was something.

4

Presley tossed the bowline to the dock boy at the local marina before waving off the Coast Guard. There was nothing else they could do for her now. She raced to the stern and handed the power cord to the other dockhand. "If I can't get power to the batteries and get the bilge pumps working, we'll have to get her out of the water sooner than the morning."

"That won't be a problem," the dockhand said. "Anything for you, Miss Presley."

"I called my buddy Kian. They're still at the hospital. Frank's wife just got there. He's been in and out of consciousness, and it's possible they need to put him in a medical coma. The burns are pretty bad. Second and third degree."

"Jesus." Presley's heart plummeted to the bottom of her gut. Fucking Vernon. Had she not had to scramble to get the damn catamaran ready, this wouldn't have happened.

It was all her fault.

Waylen tapped his cell, illuminating the flash as he studied the instrument panel and the power box. "I doubt you're going to get any power. This circuit board is fried."

"She's all plugged in, ma'am," the dock boy called.

She flipped the switch for both engines.

Nothing. Not even a hint of them turning over.

"Shit," she mumbled. "I won't be able to get my team out here until tomorrow." The bigger problem was she couldn't afford what it would cost to get this boat back in the water and it would cost a pretty penny to put it on a trailer and haul it by road back to her marina.

"It's all good, Miss Presley," the dockhand said. "You've been real good to us over the years. Your dad too. We'll take good care of you and your catamaran." He smiled. "It's late, and the roads are a little crazy because of the volcano. Might I suggest you get a room for the night. Lots of vacancies at Benny's. Kilauea has the tourists spooked. They've all cleared out. But between the wind direction and the fact it was a mild eruption with little lava flow, you should be fine."

"Thanks." She wrung out her hair before snagging her bag, which had very little. Whenever she captained a charter, she traveled light. All she needed were a few changes of underwear, shorts, and uniform shirts.

"Benny's?" Waylen offered his hand, helping her off the boat. "That's a blast from the past. Of all the places the two of us could wind up together after all these years." He waggled his brows. "Come on." He placed his hand on the small of her back. "If memory serves me correctly, this place has a small surf shop. I need to get some dry clothes. We do that, then get a couple of rooms and find some grub. I'm starving."

"You were always hungry." She laughed, patting his chest. "But you can't use the excuse you're a growing boy anymore."

"My waistline is expanding in ways that is not pleasant." He shook his head. "And I'm certainly no boy."

He pushed open the store's door and snagged a pair of shorts, a T-shirt, and a long-sleeved swim shirt. "This should do the trick, don't you think?"

"Large?" She eyed him up and down. "Boy, have you grown."

"That's just mean." He slapped his credit card on the table and paid for his items before heading out the door. "I was definitely a large when I left Big Island."

"You're fucking delusional if you believe that. You might have been tall, but you hadn't filled out.

Not like this." She paused at the corner before darting across the street. Benny's was just one block over. It wasn't a five-star hotel. Actually, it was a motel, but it was clean and run by the nicest couple. Not to mention it had been around forever. "You're looking real good, Waylen."

"You're not so bad yourself, Presley. Exactly like I remember you, feisty mouth and everything."

"First time I heard the word fuck was when you said it, so I blame you for that."

He pulled open the door to Benny's lobby. Waylen had always been a gentleman, even when they were in middle school. It was one of the many things the other kids had picked on him for. What a stupid reason to bully another child. Waylen had been the kind of boy who empathized with everyone. He had the biggest heart of anyone she'd ever met. He even cared about those teenagers who made his life difficult.

"I know that's not true." He stepped up to the counter. "Howdy, Mr. Kincaid. How are you this evening?"

"Waylen? Waylen Brown? Is that really you?" Mr. Kincaid rubbed his tired, old eyes. "Miranda. Get out here. It's Waylen and Presley. Together. Again. In our lobby." He turned and stuck his head in the back office. "Honey, did you hear me?"

"We caused quite the stir the last time we were here." She leaned against the counter.

"You mean when we got caught here?" His grin was as wide as the great state of Texas—not that she'd ever been there. The only time she'd been out of Hawaii was on her honeymoon.

Mexico.

Sun and sand.

Not much different, but she and Vernon had a good time. That first year had been filled with joy and happiness. For the first time in a long while, she thought she'd found love again. Vernon was attentive. Kind. Sweet even. They were planning for a family and a little over a year later, she found out she was pregnant. However, she miscarried right before she hit the twelve-week mark. All she had to say about that was even though that miscarriage had been emotionally and physically painful, it proved to be one of the biggest blessings that came out of her marriage. Being tied to Vernon through a child would have been the worst.

"My mother had never been more disappointed in me. My dad gave me the most uncomfortable and awkward lecture on the drive home. And your father enjoyed making me think there was a loaded shotgun behind the counter in the office." Waylen ran his hand over his mouth. "I thought he was going to beat the crap out of me every time I saw him for the next few weeks."

Waylen's hair had a few gray strands, but that

only made him sexier. He had deep-set lines around his eyes, and he'd definitely aged.

Again, that only made him more attractive.

But she'd recognize him anywhere.

This was *her* Waylen.

The one that she'd thought she'd be able to let go, but he'd lived on deep in her heart and soul.

"My parents grounded me for a week, but not because I was with you," she said. "Or what they believed we did."

"We did do the deed." He laughed. "And that's not the message that was conveyed to me."

"They were only mad that I lied to them about where I was going. It's not like they weren't already worried we might be having sex."

"We were sixteen. That's young."

"Holy crap." Mrs. Kincaid came flying out of the office and clasped her face. "It's one thing to see you, Presley. We run into you often." She ran to the other side and pulled Presley in for a big hug. "But you." She grabbed Waylen by the forearms. "Oh my. Look at you all grown-up."

"It's good to see you, Mrs. Kincaid." He leaned over and kissed her cheek. "Any chance we can get a couple of rooms for the night?"

"Two rooms?" Mrs. Kincaid looked him up and down. "I seem to remember you booking a room using an older friend's name. Having them check you in and then us having to deal with your parents."

"That was a long time ago," Presley said.

"You're not here with that crazy ex-husband of yours, are you?" Mr. Kincaid asked. "I really don't like that man."

Waylen shot her a sideways glance.

"Nope. Vernon can rot in hell for all I care," she said.

"Our sentiments exactly." Mr. Kincaid nodded. "Why don't we give you two adjoining rooms." He pushed two key cards across the counter. "Rooms five and six. On the house."

"I can't let you do that." Waylen pulled out his wallet and handed over a credit card.

"Don't insult me, boy." Mr. Kincaid waved his hand. "You two look worse for the wear. Whatever brought you here tonight, you sure look like you need a good deed."

"Thanks. We appreciate it." Waylen nodded, stuffing the key cards into his pocket. He lifted his cell and tapped on the screen.

"What are you doing?" she whispered.

"Letting my buddy Kian know where I am and what room he can find me in. I'm sure he'll show up here at some point," he said.

"Checkout is at ten, but honestly, if you need more time, just let us know," Mr. Kincaid said. "It's awfully good to see you again. Both of you."

"You as well." Waylen took Presley by the hand and tugged her toward the door.

She glanced down at their intertwined fingers. It should feel strange. Awkward. But it was the most natural thing in the world.

They still fit.

"How about we order pizza from Stallone's? They also deliver beer," she said.

"You read my mind."

"Meat lovers?" She pulled up the app on her phone.

"I like my pizza the same way I did when I was twelve, but you can get half of that veggie crap you like."

She laughed. "I'm down for some meat."

He audibly groaned as he pushed open the door to one of the rooms and waved his hand in. "I need to get out of these wet clothes."

"Me too."

"You can change in the other room or the bathroom. I'll change out here."

"Sounds like a plan." She opted for the bathroom and quickly shed her shirt and shorts, hanging them over the shower bar. She rummaged through her bag and found a tank top and pair of yoga pants.

Curling her fingers around the doorknob, she yanked it open. "Shit. Sorry."

He chuckled, hiking the shorts up over his hips. "It's not like you've never seen me in my boxers."

She swallowed, staring at scar after scar. Her father had a few from when he'd been shot, so she knew what those looked like and she counted six. Three on his stomach. Two on his thigh. One on his shoulder.

And then there were the marks snaking down his back, peeking out from under the tattoo. She had no idea what they were from, though she had a few guesses, and none of them were good.

"What a beautiful tattoo." She closed the gap, running her fingers across the colorful sailfish that spanned from one shoulder blade to the other. "How long have you had this?" She thought better of mentioning the scars.

"I started it shortly after I graduated from the Naval Academy and finished it about two years later."

"And this one." She tapped the marlin on his chest.

"High school graduation. My mom was pissed."

"Any others?"

He twisted his leg, showing off a dolphin on his right ankle and a shark on his left.

"You've always loved everything about the ocean."

"That I have," he said.

"It's so weird being here with you."

"I'll be honest. I've thought about you since the second I landed in Hawaii. But I didn't expect you to still be working for your folks. How are they?"

She threw herself back on the bed. Waylen had adored his dad and vice versa. So did her mom. They joked with her that one day she was going to marry Waylen. But not until they both finished their four-year degrees.

"Unfortunately, my mom passed of cancer eight years ago and my dad died of a heart attack about nine months after that."

"Shit, Presley. I'm so sorry." In true Waylen form, he eased onto the mattress, lifted her head, and rested it in his lap. He stroked his fingers through her hair. "I take it that's why you're back at Driftwood."

"I never really left," she admitted. "I went to college on the main island. When I finished, I came home and spent the summer like I always did, working at the marina and doing charters. I've always loved being on the water and my parents were getting older. It was harder for them to do it all and I couldn't think of anything better."

He lowered his chin. "You always wanted to travel."

"With you." She smiled. "That was your dream. You were going to join the Navy and see the world."

"We often talked about me not doing that."

She bolted upright. "No, Waylen. You talked

about giving up going to the Naval Academy and pushing off joining the Navy until after college."

"Or my bright idea of running off and getting married at eighteen and enlisting then."

"Don't remind me. That was a dumb idea." She tugged at her ponytail, running her fingers through her still damp hair.

"You ended up getting married. Tell me about him."

"Fuck no. The only thing you need to know about that prick is he's the biggest mistake I ever made."

"I've got one of those. Her name is Elena and all I've got to say is thank God she remarried so I don't have to pay alimony anymore," he said. "I've seriously got to know what your ex-husband thought of you naming one of your boats after me."

Knock. Knock.

"Saved by pizza." She stood.

He grabbed her wrist. "Oh no, you're not." He opened the door, took the takeout and the beer, and set it on the table. "No food for you until you answer the question."

"It's a sore subject and when I first did it, I just told him it was a name I liked."

"It's a fucking male name. Boats are feminine." He waggled his finger. "And if you start some bullshit about how it could be either, I'll pin you down and tickle you until you cry. I've done it before; I'll do it again."

She planted her hands on her hips. "Well, it's true. It could be a girl's name."

"Give me one example of a woman with my name."

"I can't think of one off the top of my head. But it's possible."

"When pigs fly." He cracked open a beer and handed it to her. "I don't know if I'm flattered or mortified."

"If you don't take that as a compliment, there's something seriously wrong with you."

"If you ask my ex-wife, there's a lot wrong with me." He opened the box, pulled out a slice, and stuffed half of it in his mouth before he stretched out on the bed. "Starting with the fact I kept all the letters you ever wrote me and she wasn't too pleased when she found them."

"Excuse me? How on earth did you explain keeping them?"

Waylen took a long, slow draw from his beverage. It took forever for him to finish. It was as if he was trying to finish the drink, ignore the question, or both. "I told her the truth."

"Oh, this should be good."

"All your stuff was in a box with things from Big Island, so it wasn't just your things. I had some of the music I wrote."

"Sweet Jesus." Presley smacked her hand on her forehead. "Please tell me you wrote about other girls?"

"I can't say that I've written anything since I left Big Island."

"I don't know what to say about that."

He shrugged. "I tried to express how much Big Island meant because of my dad. My memories here with him and the fact that I'm the one who found him dead. How it messed with me and how long it took me to move through all the emotions that come with grief."

"I'm sorry. While I understand I was the one holding your hand through all of that, my letters while you lived in Maryland, or your first year at the Naval Academy, have nothing to do with your father's death."

"That's pretty much what she said and that's when I told her that you were the first girl I'd ever been with. My first love. And I am my mother's son. A sentimental sap who doesn't easily part with certain things. She told me if our marriage was going to work, I needed to burn them. I refused."

"My letters were a work of art that should be cherished. Always." She took a slice and boldly climbed in next to Waylen, crossing her ankles. "But I can understand where your ex-wife would have an issue with your unwillingness to part with them. Did you divorce right after that?"

"Our relationship was bad already. She wanted things from me that I wasn't capable of, like not being a SEAL. I worked too hard to get there and I wasn't giving that up." He glanced at the sky. "I realized she went into our marriage with the idea she could *mold* or *train* me into the kind of man she thought I should be, instead of loving me for who I was. When I got assigned to a new base, I told her it was best if we parted ways. I believe her last words to me were to go find my little slut, meaning you."

"I've been called worse." She laughed. "My ex-husband thinks I'm classless."

"He's a dick." Waylen raised his beer.

"Too bad his penis is the size of my pinky."

Waylen coughed, spewing half his sip across the room. "I hope you weren't going around saying shit like that about me when you dumped my ass."

"Seriously, that's how you're going to play this? Because I didn't break up with you. I simply suggested that we both focus on our studies."

"And then you stopped writing."

"So did you."

"I got the impression that's what you wanted," he said. "I have the letter if you want me to find it and read it to you."

"Ouch, that hurt." She narrowed her stare. "After two and a half years, I didn't want to be the girl who held you back." She covered his mouth with her hand. She'd waited twenty-three years to say some of this and while she had no intention of being completely honest at this point, she would give him a healthy dose of some of it. "The few times we talked, I could hear how much you loved the Academy. How you thrived in the environment and how honored and proud you knew your dad would have been."

"All of that is true. But that doesn't mean I wanted to stop—"

"I'm not saying that's what I wanted either. But circumstances as they were, it was what was best for both of us."

He burst out laughing.

"I don't know what the hell is so funny."

"You're divorced. You named a fucking boat after me. We're sitting in a motel room, where we both lost our virginity to one another. You ordered my favorite pizza instead of that stupid veggie shit you like and were always trying to push on me. You're trying like hell not to rip my clothes off. Come on, Presley. You're still hung up on me."

She poked him dead center on his chest. "I'm not the one who kept love letters from some teenage girl from twenty-three fucking years ago and let my spouse read them. And I didn't name the boat after you. I named it after my cat."

"There is a cat named Waylen?"

She shrugged. "I like the name. What's wrong with that?"

"Oh, let me count the ways." He sighed. "Anything else about me you're hanging on to? Like, is my name tattooed on your body?"

She cringed. "No."

"Jesus. Is it?"

"I swear to God, it's not."

"What the hell did you do, Presley? Show me." He plucked the beer from her hands and glared. "Don't make me go looking."

"Fine." She lifted her shirt and rolled down her pants, exposing her hip and a heart tattoo with the date of their first time together.

He leaned closer, squinting. "We have to be two of the most pathetic people on this planet."

"Speak for yourself."

"I am." He handed her beer back. "I never once stopped thinking about you."

"That's nice to hear." She took a long swig of her beer. "I suppose first loves are always the ones you never forget. But maybe that's why they are firsts and not lasts."

"I don't know. According to my ex-wife, I never loved her and you know what? I think she's right about that. I believe I was in love with the idea of her, but never her."

"That's just cruel."

"I guess it is," he said. "What about you and this Vernon guy?"

"He had me snowed, the fucking con artist."

"Why don't you tell me how you really feel?"

"No. That wouldn't be ladylike." She held his stare with her heart hammering in her throat. "Then again, neither is this." Straddling him, she cupped his face and pressed her mouth over his, slipping her tongue between his lips.

God, he tasted so good. It was like she'd found her own private meal in heaven.

His fingers dug into her thighs as he deepened the kiss.

Her lungs filled with thick anticipation. This wasn't a trip down memory lane. A reliving of the past.

This wasn't the boy she'd fallen in love with when she'd been a teenager. He was a man now. A man who'd seen the world. Been married. Divorced. And Lord only knew what else.

No matter how much of the Waylen she knew she could see in his eyes, he'd changed.

And so had she.

She wasn't the same young girl who dreamed about getting off Big Island and seeing what the rest of the world had to offer. She knew how good she had it right where she'd lived her entire life.

His touch was hauntingly familiar and yet so new and different. His kisses were as sweet as they'd ever been. But his passion was more intense. Wild.

And definitely more wicked.

His ability to remove her clothes without fumbling was impressive.

She surrendered to him, letting go of any lingering doubts or reservations. The past was just that—the past. What mattered now was the blazing fire between them, igniting with every touch and every kiss. Their bodies moved together in a dance of desire, a symphony of longing that had been with her for years.

As her skin met his, every nerve ending came alive, sending shivers down her spine. The way he explored her body with such reverence and hunger made her feel like she was the only woman in the world. In that moment, nothing else existed but the two of them, lost in a timeless embrace.

And as they reached the peak of their passion, she knew that this wasn't just a fleeting moment of reunion. It was a reawakening of something deep and primal that had always been between them, waiting to be unleashed.

The deep love she'd always had for him matured and evolved, weathered by time and distance but stronger than ever. And as they lay intertwined in each other's arms, she knew that the connection they shared transcended the boundaries of age, experience, and the past.

The world around them faded into a blur, as if they were the only two souls on earth. The room seemed to shrink and the bed expanded, becoming a place of endless possibilities.

Their eyes locked once more, revealing the depths of their newfound passion. But something else lingered in his gaze. Confusion. A question. Perhaps concern or even doubt. He pulled her closer. "This is probably not the right moment to mention this, but are you on birth control?"

"Shit," she mumbled. "No, and that's something we should have discussed before you ripped my clothes off."

"It's always amazed me the selective memory you have because you started this." He kissed her nose. "Not that I'm complaining."

She wrapped her arms around his strong body, nuzzling her face into his neck. "I'm almost forty. This isn't the kind of mistake I should be making at my age."

"We can't go back and correct it, so we'll have to deal with it. There's nothing else we can do right at this moment." He reached behind him, flicked off the light, and tugged the covers over their naked bodies. "We're both tired. It's late. Let's discuss it in the morning."

"Easy for you to say. If the sperm does meet the egg, it's not happening inside your body."

He pressed his mouth against the top of her head and laughed.

"It's not funny."

"I'm not laughing at the situation, but the verbiage you chose. I mean, really. I got detention at least half a dozen times for cracking up over the things that came out of your mouth." He cupped her face, pressing his warm lips over hers. "I get it. I'm not thrilled with my level of disrespect because I was too busy enjoying myself. But that doesn't change that at two in the morning, we can't do a damn thing about it. Let's get a few hours of sleep, and we can go from there. It's not like we're sixteen and our parents are going to come busting through that door."

"That was so embarrassing."

"For everyone."

She snuggled in, resting her head on his chest, draping her arm and leg across his body.

A perfect fit.

And yet, it was all going to end.

Again.

5

Waylen stared at the ceiling.

Gently, he ran his fingers through Presley's hair, sprawled across his chest. He remembered the first time he woke with her in his arms. It had been the most natural thing back then, and nothing had changed.

Only, this morning, there was a more incredible heaviness in his chest.

After his father died, he'd suspected his mom had plans to move back to Maryland. He thought she would wait for him to graduate from high school. But she couldn't stand to be surrounded by all the things that his dad loved so much.

Hawaii had become their home. His father intended to retire and stay forever, and his mother was completely on board.

However, all that had changed in a flash, leaving

Waylen heartbroken, not only over the death of his dad, but over leaving behind the girl he'd fallen in love with.

This morning, he knew he'd have to say goodbye once again, maybe not today or even tomorrow.

She groaned and stretched. "What time is it?"

"Close to eight," he whispered.

"Holy shit. I never sleep that late."

"You needed the rest." He brushed his lips over her forehead, taking in her fresh, sweet strawberry scent. She always smelled so good.

She rolled, reaching for her phone. "My crew should be at the marina by nine. I need to be there when they arrive."

"I haven't heard from Kian or how I'm getting back to the Brotherhood Protectors ranch." He fluffed the pillow, pushing to a sitting position. "I might not be working for them, but I'm sure they could use my help in other locations. Kilauea has been rumbling all night."

"I know. I heard her a few times. At least the alarm didn't go off."

"She's the only thing I haven't missed about this island."

Presley rested her chin on his chest, her fingers dancing across his skin. "I blinked open my eyes a couple of times in the middle of the night. I still can't believe you're here. Or that you were in Blake's chopper and the one to come rescue me."

"That was wild." He leaned over, giving her a proper kiss good morning. "My mom is going to be happy that we ran into each other. From the second I set foot in Hawaii, she's been asking me if I've gotten in touch with any of my old friends, but especially you."

"I'm not hard to find."

"I noticed your driver's license. You no longer have the same last name."

"That's something that I need to change. I've been divorced for three years. I hate signing that fucker's last name."

"You really don't like your ex."

"Not one little bit."

"I'm sorry that you had a shitty time of it with him," he said.

"There were so many warning signs, and I chose to ignore them early on. I wanted to be married, to have a family. And in the beginning, he was sweet and kind. He had me totally snowed."

He lifted her chin. "You've always been able to see the good in people. That's not a flaw."

"With him, it was."

"Do you have kids?" he asked, but he wasn't sure he wanted to know the answer.

"We tried. I had one miscarriage early in our marriage, and then I never got pregnant again. It was for the best. As much as I would have loved being a mom, being tied to that prick through a child for the rest of my life would be an even bigger hell than having to deal with him the way I do now," she said. "What about you?"

"Another bone of contention between me and Elena."

"Why? Who didn't want kids?"

"We both wanted them, but I kept putting her off. My career was dangerous. I was deployed all the time, and I wasn't willing to give it up yet. That pissed her off and frankly, I don't blame her. However, the reality is, looking back, I don't think I wanted them with her because, deep down, I knew we weren't right for each other."

"How long have you been out of the Navy?"

"A few months," he admitted. "I'm starting to get bored. Me and my buddies have been traveling. We're all looking for the next thing. It's not like we're that old, but we're not sure what to do next."

"What about the organization that brought you to Hawaii?"

"The Brotherhood Protectors isn't what brought us here. We came for a retirement party. But they have offices here and in other places around the United States. And even internationally. It's an option. But whatever we decide, we go as a team. We're family."

"All of you?"

"You'll understand when you meet them."

"Tell me about them. This band of brothers of yours."

"That's a perfect descriptor for them." He chuckled. "We've been through hell and back together. Nearly died on missions. Saw some of our comrades fall. I don't know if I could have survived half of what the military tossed my way if it weren't for them. Much less life in general. Each one brings something unique to the table. Take Lane for example. He's one of my best friends. He and I share a passion for surfing."

"Oh, good Lord. You're not very good."

"I've gotten better, thanks to Lane." Waylen arched a brow. "But Lane lost his mom, something we've bonded over. He understands more than anyone what I've been through. He knows when to give me space or when I need to talk just by looking at me. Raider, he's the explosives expert in the group. He can tell when I need a joke and he always delivers the right one at the right moment. Almost always completely inappropriate, but that's what I adore about that man."

"He sounds interesting."

"Oh, he is. But you should meet Harlan. He's the negotiator. Annoying as fuck sometimes. However, the man has a heart of gold and he manages to say and do the right thing every time." Waylen smiled. "That leaves Kian. He's truly my best friend. A male soulmate, if you will. He's a little pissed off at me right now because I never told him about you until last night, but he'll get over it because at the end of the day, he understands me more than anyone. I've never had friends like these four. They're loyal. Honorable. And whatever happens next, we'll do it together." That statement made this next part of the conversation that much harder. He let out a long breath. "We've been searching for whatever that is, but we haven't found it yet."

She patted his chest. "I have no doubt you will."

"That brings me to what I've been thinking about for the last forty minutes, waiting for you to wake up." He kissed her nose. "Shall we talk about what happened last night, the fact we didn't use protection and what that means?"

"It doesn't necessarily mean anything." She sat up, pulling the covers up over her body. "I didn't use birth control for six years, and it never happened."

"That doesn't mean it won't happen now."

"I'll be forty next month. I'm a little old to be worried about that."

"That's bullshit and you're avoiding." He arched a brow. "This bothered you last night, but I brushed you off."

"There's the morning-after pill, if I can find it. And there are other options if we find ourselves in that position. But it's also not your problem." She rolled over.

He yanked her to his chest. "Don't you dare try to tell me I have no responsibility in this. Or try to walk away from me. If you do find yourself pregnant, we both had something to do with it and we'll both decide what steps to take."

"Why? You just said you and your friends will be leaving because you all decide together what you're doing."

"For fuck's sake, that's not what I said." He ran a hand over his mouth. "I have no idea what's next. Only…" Shit. He had implied that. "Look. I'm a little freaked out over a few things right now. But I don't regret being with you. Not even a little bit. And what should have me panicked beyond belief doesn't have me wanting to run out of this room and off this island."

She jerked her head. "I'm not even sure what to do with that statement."

"I'm not either." He tucked a few strands of hair behind her ear. "I wasn't sure about coming to Big Island and not because of my father. I used that as an excuse. Sure, I miss him every fucking day of my life. I can't ever erase the moment I found him lying on the kitchen floor."

"Oh, Waylen. I know." She palmed his cheek.

"But my bigger reason for not wanting to return was you." He curled his fingers around her wrist.

"The memories of you. What they stir up in me. All the questions of what could have been. Don't you ever think about that?"

"Of course I do," she whispered. "But that's a dangerous road to go down." She lowered her gaze. "And the reality is you loved your career. Don't try to tell me you didn't."

"I won't. I did love everything about it. I thrived in the Navy. As a SEAL. I know it's what I was born to do." He lifted a finger and swiped away a tear that rolled down the side of her face. "But that doesn't mean I don't wonder what my life would have been like if I had the chance to share it with you."

"That's a sweet thought. I appreciate it. But we were kids."

"Who wholeheartedly loved each other."

"I won't deny that. However, it was over twenty years ago." She covered his mouth. "Can we please just enjoy this time we have together? I understand there may be a consequence to it, but I don't want that to ruin this moment." She dropped her hand.

"That's a reasonable request."

"Thank you."

She pulled back the covers, stood, and lifted her shirt, pulling it over her head.

"Aw, come on. Why'd you have to go do that? I was enjoying the view." He waggled his finger.

"Your boobs got bigger." If she wanted to rejoice in this time, he would bask in it.

"You told me you liked my itty-bitty ones." She smiled.

"I did. But I think I like the full mature ones better." He winked.

"You're a pig." She laughed. "I need to go shower."

"I have a condom in my wallet. Can I join you if I bring it?"

She glared. "Where was that when we needed it last night?"

"I got lost in your sexiness." He shrugged.

"Fine, but only if you sing for me."

"I haven't sung in years."

"Why not? You have a beautiful voice. Especially when it's belting out that Meatloaf song."

"All right, but you have to promise to sing your part."

"Oh, I'll sing, but you have to get me there first." She wadded up her yoga pants and tossed them at his face. "Are you up for the challenge, sailor?"

"You know I—"

Knock. Knock.

"Who the fuck is that?" She jumped on the bed, snagged her pants, and shimmied her adorable ass into them.

"Knowing Mr. and Mrs. Kincaid, they're prob-

ably bringing us room service or something."
Waylen found his shorts and hiked them up over his
hips. He strolled to the door and yanked it open,
scratching the top of his head. "Good morning—
Kian? Why didn't you text or call?"

Kian shifted his gaze between Waylen and Presley. "I was banging on the other door for the last ten
minutes. You know, the one you said you'd be in, but
when you didn't answer, I thought I'd try the one
you said Presley would be in." He pushed past
Waylen.

Blake followed. "Hey, Presley."

"Blake," Presley said.

"So, this is the infamous Presley." Kian shoved a
to-go mug at Waylen. "I wish I could say I've heard
all about you, but I just learned of your existence
last night. It is, however, a pleasure to meet you."
Gently, he handed her the other cup.

"Waylen, huh?" Blake took a seat at the small
table. "I always knew there was a story behind that
name. I just never thought he'd be so handsome."
She looked him up and down. "Holy shit. He's the
guy in the picture. I knew he looked familiar."

"What picture?" Waylen asked.

"The one Al and Lisa have of us at the bar at
the marina."

"I was a scrawny teenager," Waylen mumbled.
"They still have that up?"

Presley nodded. "You and your dad too."

"Lucy, you have some explaining to do," Kian said. "Keeping secrets from me." He shook his head. "But all that is going to have to wait. Lane texted. So did Hawk. We're needed at The Resort. ASAP. Blake's been so kind as to offer us a lift."

"Last time I climbed into a chopper with Miss Gardenia over there, I got shoved out into the water. I'm not sure I want to do that again. Not unless I know Presley's the one who needs saving." Waylen looped his arm around Presley. "And since she's going to be on land, I kind of want to pass."

"You know that's not an option." Kian cocked a brow. "You'd really leave Lane hanging?"

"For Presley, I might consider it." Waylen lifted his chin. "But if you ever tell him that, I'll deny it."

"Damn, that's cold." Kian gave Waylen a good shove.

"Why the hell is he calling me Gardenia? I'm no flower," Blake said. "I take offense to that."

"Don't," Waylen said. "I'm only referring to the image on your bird. That's all. And it's better than the nickname I gave Kian when I first met him."

"Oh, this should be good." Presley folded her arms. "Do tell."

"He's so full of shit. Don't listen to him," Kian said.

"No. I want to hear this. He's notorious for handing out nicknames. When we first met, he kept calling me Cilla. As in short for Priscilla."

"As in Priscilla Presley?" Blake asked. "That's cute."

"I hated it." Presley pursed her lips. "So, what did you call Kian?"

"Most people translate Kian into God. Or King. No fucking way was I calling him that. It would go straight to his head. But one of the other translations can be Ancient. So, I just called him that for the first year we met because he's also a couple of days older than me."

"You're a jackass, is what you are," Kian mumbled. "Sorry, Presley. But we need to hit the friendly skies. Duty calls."

She waved her hands. "I get it. No worries."

"Give us a minute, will you?" Waylen shoved Kian out the door. He nodded at Blake. He wasn't about to give her a nudge with his hands. She scared him.

"Sure thing. We'll be outside." Blake followed Kian out the door.

Waylen slammed it shut. "Sorry I can't join you in the shower." He cupped her face, giving her a sweet kiss. "I'll call you when I'm done with whatever Lane needs help with, okay?"

Presley nodded.

"We can spend a little time together before I head off to wherever I'm going next."

"I'd like that." She leaned into him, kissing him

hard. "Be safe out there, and don't get yourself killed in the process."

"I won't." He snagged his shirt, tugging it over his head, and gripped the door. He glanced over his shoulder. "Hey. Please, whatever you decide to do about the morning-after pill, tell me. I understand it's your body and I respect that. But I want to know either way. I'd like to be in on the discussion."

"I promise I'll call you."

"Thank you." He sucked in a deep breath and yanked open the door. He didn't know what felt worse.

The day he boarded the plane for Maryland when he was seventeen, or this moment, knowing it could be as life-altering as that move had been.

6

---

*P*resley dipped her feet into the cool water and stared at the horizon. The volcano rumbled angrily in the background, and ash clouds floated out over the ocean. She'd gone to the local drugstore down the road.

No Plan B.

She should be upset. Scared. Concerned. Angry. Something. Anything other than slightly relieved.

But she wasn't.

It was now two days since she'd slept with Waylen and past the time she could even take the pill.

She lifted her cell and found Waylen's contact information. She'd made him a promise and she intended to honor it.

And she wouldn't do it in a text. He deserved much better than that.

Before tapping the call button, she glanced over her shoulder. Tim, her engineer, Tony, the marina's mechanic, Remi, and a special investigator were all in the catamaran up on the dry dock, working on learning what had caused the minor explosion.

She hated using that term; however, that's precisely what had transpired.

The phone rang twice.

"Hey, Presley. What's up?" Waylen asked.

"How are things at The Resort?"

"Honestly, hectic. I don't have much time between this and a situation going on with both Harlan and Raider. But it's damn good to hear your voice."

Jesus, that melted her heart right down to her fucking toes. Waylen shouldn't make her feel like she was the only woman in his world. What they shared was a trip down memory lane. It was a chance for them to say all the things they hadn't when his mom ripped him from Big Island without warning.

It should represent closure.

Not a new beginning.

She shouldn't confuse the two.

"I wanted to touch base with you about our little situation," she said.

"Is everything okay? Are you okay?"

"I'm still staying at Benny's. My team is taking a while to assess the damage. An investigator is here and trying to determine exactly what happened.

There aren't many drugstores around here, and I was unable to find the morning-after pill. I tried, but we'll have to wait this one out."

"I understand," he said. "How do you feel about that?"

Being brutally honest with him might be too much for both of them. It didn't matter that he'd poured his heart out. He never said he'd stay. Not once did he mention being a father. Or even co-parenting. All he did was let her know that he'd be around to 'deal with it,' and she feared that meant something else.

But she didn't know because she hadn't asked.

She couldn't blame him if that's what he wanted. There were so many good reasons for not having a child. They weren't all that young anymore. They didn't know each other either. They had a past, which included a loving relationship. But that didn't make for a future.

"I have mixed emotions about it all," she said.

Some things in life are worth risking everything. You'll know it in your heart, feel it in your bones, and question it because it will force you to bear your soul, and it's possible that you could lose everything. But you'll never know unless you put it out there.

Those were her father's wise words.

Perhaps she needed to put something out in the universe. The Waylen she knew was contemplative, weighing all his options. While he was an emotional man, he based his decisions in logic.

It wouldn't be fair if she kept her true thoughts to herself.

"If by chance the craziest thing has happened, it certainly wouldn't be the way I wanted to have a child, being single. But a child is something I've always wanted. Something I've always dreamed about."

Crickets.

She waited for a good minute for him to say something, but no words came.

"Waylen?"

"I'm here," he said. "I'm searching for the right words."

"Silence speaks volumes."

"No. Actually, it doesn't. Not when you can't see my face to gauge my response," he said. "This is hard over the phone for that reason. It's also hard because I'm not you. I'm not a woman. And to be frank, I gave up on the idea of having a family years ago. When Elena and I divorced, I swore off ever getting married again. Or even a committed relationship. And kids were certainly out of the equation."

"You wouldn't have to be part of—"

"First, you're putting the cart before the horse. And second, you know me better than that," he said. "It's not that I'm afraid of this. You don't have me running scared. It's just that I'm at a crossroads in my life in general. Seeing you again has brought so many things to the surface. I care about you. I always have. I always will. And I want to spend more time with you. I feel as though we were cheated out of something."

"I feel a but coming on."

"No buts. It's just a lot of what-ifs and I don't do well with them. We wait it out and not worry about it until we know. Then we talk. I'm not going anywhere in terms of support. I also don't want to lose you again. I don't know what that means for a lot of reasons."

"Crossroads."

"It's more than that, Presley, and it's not something that can be hashed out over the phone," he said. "I'm sorry, but I'm going to have to hang up shortly. Things here are complicated. I'm working on three different missions at once. Hopefully things here will wrap up in a day or two and I'll meet you wherever you are, okay?"

"All right."

"Hey, before I go. Has the investigator mentioned anything to you about the boat?"

It had been a long while since she had someone in her life who took the time to check in on her and her problems. Blake did it. Remi and his wife were always looking out for her. A few of her other employees who had been around a long while also took the time. But Vernon had fractured some of her relationships. She'd also built up walls. He'd broken her trust and her spirit.

"He's going through the vessel. I'm hoping I'll know exactly what happened by the end of the day, but he hasn't given me any indication of what he's thinking yet."

"This wasn't your fault, Presley."

"You can say that all you want and trust me, I appreciate you trying to make me feel better. But that cat was due for service. I had no business taking it out."

"Your ex-husband forced your hand. And any number of things could have gone wrong. You know that. So stop beating yourself up."

"I can't. There's a man in the hospital fighting for his life." She swiped at her cheeks. From the moment the fire broke out, she knew she did everything right. Hell, once the volcano erupted and she decided to go to the dock instead of picking up a buoy and continuing with the charter, she'd been making all the right moves. But it didn't change the outcome.

"Babe, until you have answers, you need to stop making yourself crazy."

Her heart swelled. Waylen used to call her *babe* when they were dating, but he hadn't used it until now, and it made all the difference in the world.

"I promise I'll be back in touch as soon as I can to help you with all this."

"You're busy, and I understand the stakes. I do. There are lots of crazy things going on around Big Island. Do what you need to with your buddies. You're helping good people. I've met Cassie and the family she protects. What went down is insane."

"Cassie mentioned they went on a Driftwood Tours. She sang your praises," Waylen said. "So did the family. I've got a few things to do to wrap that up, along with dealing with the situation with Raider and some IT work for Harlan. There are rumblings that we'll have to go back to the ranch for a debrief before I can get to you."

"There's no reason for you to rush. I'm not in any danger. What you're dealing with is far more pressing," she said. "Be safe."

"I will. Talk soon."

She couldn't be angry with him for anything he said. He was right. There was no point in discussing what might be until they knew for sure, and she shouldn't worry about things she couldn't control, including what the inspector might find. Waylen was saying and doing all the right things. He was present and he wasn't blowing smoke up her skirt.

He wasn't Vernon.

Waylen was a kind and caring man. He wouldn't simply walk out of her life and leave her hanging. He didn't do that twenty-three years ago.

That hadn't been his choice and it had been she who slowly cut off communication, ending what had already been destroyed by distance.

Waylen leaned back and cracked his knuckles. Between the phone call with Presley and staring at a fucking tiny computer screen for the last five hours, his brain was fried.

Knock. Knock.

He stood, peering out the peephole.

Lane.

Opening the door, he plastered on his best smile. "What's up, man?"

"You look like death," Lane said.

"You don't look much better." Waylen chuckled. "Been a hell of a few days."

"Damn straight." Lane fell back onto the sofa by the sliding glass doors. He raked a hand through his hair. "What are you working on?"

"Background checks for Harlan. Deep dives for Raider. And my own little project that has me wanting to blow out someone's kneecap."

"Damn. That's aggressive for the quiet computer geek who prefers to spend his time fishing or surfing by himself."

Waylen chuckled. "Take a look at this." He handed Lane a computer printout.

"Wow. You're looking up the ex-girlfriend's ex-husband. There's a word for that, but I'm going to choose not to use it until you tell me why you're doing it." Lane held up the paper. His eyes shifted left to right, but his face remained expressionless. "It's not uncommon for spouses to split business in a divorce. If one can't afford to buy out the other—"

"I haven't given you the full picture." Waylen wanted another night with Presley. No. He wanted many nights with her and if he were being totally honest with himself, the idea of staying on Big Island had become more than a concept.

It was now something he wanted.

Not because there was a remote chance that Presley could be pregnant. They had sex once. Granted, it only took once, and he'd never taken that risk before. Ever. But he wanted to know if what he and Presley had was still real, and the only way to know was to spend time together.

Real time.

Besides, being back on Big Island was like coming home. It was the first time in his adult life that being in any one spot made him feel grounded.

"I'm listening," Lane said.

"I've known Presley and her family my entire life. Her dad was incredibly protective of her and he wanted to make sure Driftwood Tours was a healthy business to leave to his daughter."

"And was it?"

"Not when he died." Waylen unplugged his computer, set it on his lap, and found the financial files. He shouldn't have gone poking around Presley's business and when she found out, she was going to have something to say about it.

"Was Presley married when he died?"

Waylen nodded. "Vernon got almost half when they divorced."

"That seems like a lot for a brief marriage."

"It does. But at the time, she was the breadwinner, and the reasons for it aren't important," Waylen said. "Before her father died, her mom had taken ill, and Vernon got involved in the business while Presley and her dad attended to her mother."

"I take it he made some bad decisions."

"Bad is being kind," Waylen said. "It started with cutting corners on safety things on the boats. Or quality scuba and snorkeling equipment. There are complaints regarding the food on charters. Two new boats were bought before the older ones were retired, putting a strain on the business. And then there were special charters. Ones that went off course."

"What do mean by that?" Lane glanced over the papers.

"Didn't go to where the charters had stated. And they were all done by captains that weren't employees, but hired through other means," Waylen said. "That's done sometimes when people go on vacations, but these seemed strange."

"As in, you believe something else could have been happening?" Lane arched a brow. "Like smuggling?"

"That's where my mind went. But there's more. There are also discounted charters for what were listed as special VIP guests. Some of them match those charters that went off course. Others, the fares were so discounted that it doesn't make sense. All of them have her ex-husband's name next to them. I've hacked into all the financials and on the surface, it looks like bad management on his part. But it doesn't feel that way to me." He handed Lane the computer. "It looks more like skimming off the top."

"Do you know how much money we're talking?"

"It's a fair amount. A few hundred grand over a two-year period," Waylen said. "Also, one of the new boats was sold right after it was purchased. Not necessarily a red flag, especially if they couldn't afford to keep it. But it got me thinking about money laundering."

"Why? What does this Vernon guy do?"

"A whole lot of fucking nothing." Waylen took his computer back and tapped a few keystrokes. "This is Vernon. He might as well be a snake oil salesman."

Lane took the laptop and stared at the screen.

"He says here that he's been a time-share salesman, a used car salesman, and a high-risk investment broker."

"While he is part owner in Driftwood Tours, he also has a stake in a car wash, a dog grooming and boarding business, to name a few. That's suspicious to me."

"Don't get pissed, but that's in part because you've got the hots for this girl." Lane handed the computer back. "What do her books look like now?"

"Since the divorce, it's been perfect. She managed a controlling interest in the settlement, but what baffles me is how he got close to half in a seven-year marriage."

"You had to pay alimony and your marriage wasn't very long."

"That happened for two reasons. She quit her job twice to move with me and I offered until she got her feet on the ground. I didn't know she was going to take my kindness and turn it against me."

"Which is why you took a piano that you don't even know how to play." Lane chuckled.

If the man only knew the instrumental talents Waylen possessed. "I was pissed. She bought the damn thing because it looked pretty in the family room and even she can't play the stupid thing, so I took it out of principle. But that's not the point. You're comparing apples to oranges. The alimony she was awarded would have run out in a couple of years. It was a small amount. This man has owner-ship in a business that his name was never on."

"If there's no prenup, nothing can be done."

"I'm honestly surprised that she didn't have one." Waylen set the laptop on the desk. "She told me that Vernon offered to buy her out when they got divorced."

"That's bold."

"The whole thing bothers the fuck out of me."

"What are you planning on doing about it?"

He leaned back, clasping his hands behind his head. "The guy injured on Presley's boat is a busi-ness associate of Vernon's. Until I know more about their relationship and get the investigator's report, nothing, except maybe call in a favor from an old friend to tail Vernon."

"Who?" Lane stood.

"This guy I went to high school with. His name's Mano. He's a private dick these days. I sent him what I have on Vernon. He doesn't have his sights on him yet, but he will."

"Do what you must and let me know how I can help. In the meantime, pack up. We need to head back to Hawk's ranch for a meeting today. Blake's offered us a ride." Lane shook his head. "I don't think I've ever seen Kian so smitten before. He's like a lovesick puppy."

"You're one to talk with Cassie. You're like a fast car speeding down the highway."

Lane smiled. "Shut up." He tried to wipe the grin off his face but failed miserably. He waggled his finger. "And don't you dare toss out that stupid nickname."

When they first met, two things stuck out about Lane. He often didn't stay in his own lane and he drove like a crazy motherfucker, which is why Waylen called him Tracy. "Okay, Tracy." Without overthinking about what he was doing, Waylen sang one of the lines from "Fast Car" by Tracy Chapman.

Lane did a double take. "You can carry a tune?"

"Can't everyone?"

"Hell no." Lane narrowed his eyes. "How is it that I never knew you could sing."

"Because I can't." He rose, stuffing his computer into his backpack. "Not really, anyway. Give me five to finish getting my shit together. I'll meet you in the lobby."

"Sounds good." Lane disappeared into the hallway, leaving Waylen with his thoughts.

They drifted off to his dad as they often did.

He pulled out his cell. "Hey Siri, call Mom."

It rang once. "Hey, Waylen. How are you? How's Presley?"

"I'm good. So is she." He chuckled. No way would he get into the details of what was really going on with his mother. She worried enough about him as it was. The last thing he needed was for her to add Presley to the mix and for his mom to get all hopeful about that. "I haven't been able to spend any time with her these last few days because of work for her and, of course, helping out with the Brotherhood Protectors and their aid in the eruption of Kilauea."

"I can't believe she spewed while you were there," his mom said. "I guess that was her way of welcoming you home."

"Funny you should mention that." He strolled into the bathroom and collected his toiletries. "The guys and I have been talking about what we want to do next and we keep coming back to working for the Brotherhood Protectors."

"Seriously?"

"We don't know if it's an option yet, but it's a great organization. The men and women we've met so far are top-notch, and they have branches in Montana, Colorado, West Yellowstone, and here, to name a few."

"Where do you think you'd end up?"

"That's a good question. The goal would be here, but that's up to the Hawk and Hank," Waylen said. "If it even happens. But I wanted to ask you if I did move back here, how would you feel about that and would you come with me?"

"Are you serious?"

"Of course I am," he said. "But for now, it's

purely a hypothetical question. I'm just gauging your emotions. I know it might not be easy for you."

"This is all about a job? And nothing to do with Presley?"

He took his toiletry kit and stuffed it in his rucksack. He was prepared for this question.

"I can't live off my retirement forever. It's not enough and I'm too young. I need to work and the Brotherhood Protectors is the kind of outfit that would give me and the boys the kind of work we enjoy minus being shot at all the time." He opted not to tell his mother that had already happened.

Twice.

"I wasn't sure about coming back because of all the memories of Dad, but instead of making me feel sad about him being gone, it's made me feel closer to him."

"I'm glad about that," she said. "But are you sure it doesn't have to do with Presley? Are you positive that's not the driving force?"

Jesus. She was like a dog with a bone. "It's been great seeing Presley again. We're enjoying catching up and talking about old times." Putting the cell on speaker, he hoisted his rucksack and tossed it over his shoulder while reaching for his backpack.

His mom giggled. "Have you and Presley hooked up?"

He dropped his bag on his foot.

"Fuck," he mumbled, hopping around on one leg.

"Language, son."

"Sorry, Ma. But really? Whatever gave you that idea? I told you what happened. The event that surrounded me even seeing her again." He sat on the edge of the bed and rubbed his temples. Not once had he given her the impression that anything had transpired. Nor would he. She would be planning their wedding if he had.

"Oh, a little birdie might have given me some details about that night."

"What the heck does that mean?"

"I got a phone call from Mrs. Kincaid and she might have mentioned that you and Presley spent the night at Benny's. In one room."

He smacked his forehead. "For the record, I got two rooms."

"But you didn't use both," his mom said in that singsong voice she used when she wanted to tease him while making a point. "She also might have mentioned seeing the two of you in an intimate embrace—"

"I really don't want to talk about this with you."

"So, it's true. You spent the night with Presley," she said with a fair amount of triumph in her tone.

No way was he going to admit it. But if he kept denying it, she'd keep pressing on. His mother didn't know when to quit regarding certain things in his life, especially Presley. When he and Elena divorced, the first thing out of his mother's mouth was that he should look Presley up. "Mom. Would you consider moving back to Big Island if I took a job with the Brotherhood Protectors or not?"

"I always thought you and Presley would make some gorgeous children and I'd love to be a grandma."

"Mother, this isn't about me and Presley. It's about a job and whether or not you will move like we talked about. I want you close to me."

"I hate it when you call me that, young man, and to answer your question, yes. I would. But in part because Presley's there and I like the idea of the two of you getting back together. I've always felt a pang of guilt for taking you away from that girl. I'd hoped that after you got settled in the Navy, she'd find her way back to you. Instead, you wound up with Elena."

He pinched the bridge of his nose. "I've had a good life, Mom. A happy one. I have no regrets."

"Maybe not. But there's always been something missing and her name's Presley."

"I love you, Ma. But you've got to stop with this Presley thing, okay? Even if there is something brewing, and I'm not saying there is, there are no guarantees. We're completely different people."

"That gives me a little hope," she said. "I know I

say this a lot, but your dad, he'd be so proud of the man you've become."

"That's because a good woman raised me."

"Oh, now I know there's something you're not telling me," she said. "But you can keep your little secret for now."

"I'll talk to you soon."

"I love you, Waylen."

He tapped the red button on his cell. "Good Lord." He shook his head. For all his life he could never keep a secret, tell a lie, or hide anything from his mother. She had this weird sense of knowing exactly what was going on with him, sometimes before he knew.

This situation was no different.

Only, he wasn't sure how to handle it all.

7

Presley gripped the report that Hale Pau, the investigator, had completed between her shaky fingers. To her right, the *Waylen* sat on a trailer in dry dock. The fire had damaged her starboard hull. The circuit board and electronics for the navigation system, among other things, needed to be replaced.

"Your vessel is now a crime scene," Hale said. "We appreciate yours and Remi's statements. But we'll need anyone else to also give a statement who had access to the catamaran before it set sail."

"I'm happy to provide you a list." She glanced at the sheet of paper.

Gas leak.

Specifically, the gas line had been tampered with.

As well as the generator, which they had been lucky worked the first couple of nights.

"Most of my people are back near The Resort. My entire base of operation is at the marina right next door." She waved the document. "May I keep this?"

"Yes, ma'am. It's for your records." Hale nodded. "You mentioned that you live above your office and lost power the night before the charter."

"The entire marina did."

"For how long?" Hale asked.

"About forty-five minutes."

"Why didn't the generator kick in?"

"There was a coolant leak." She shrugged. "Topper had it serviced three months ago. I know that to be a fact because I called the company and was there the day they came. The generator isn't that old, so it doesn't make sense. But Topper fixed it immediately, and it appears to be working fine now."

"I've had a chance to speak with Melissa and she's reported that neither she nor her husband have any enemies. What about you?" Hale looped his fingers into his belt.

"The only person who has a beef with me is my ex-husband, Vernon."

"Your business partner?" Hale lowered his chin.

"It wasn't a very good marriage, and the divorce got ugly," she admitted. "Lucky for him at the time, my business was making more than his. Then, to add insult to injury for me, his main source of income went belly up. He got partial ownership in my family's blood, sweat, and tears. I'm working my ass off to buy him out. Especially now that he's come into money."

"No offense, ma'am, but you sound bitter."

"That's because I am. When Vernon and I got married, my folks were still alive. That business was theirs and they never intended for him to have any piece of it. My father warned me about not having a prenup."

"Has your ex ever threatened you? Was he abusive in any way?"

"No to both questions," she admitted. "About the worst I can accuse him of outside of being a prick is he cheated on me once, and he could be cruel."

"Cruel how?"

"If he got pissed off, he'd tell me I looked fat. Or blame me for the miscarriage that I suffered. He told me that if I had been a better wife and cared for him better, he wouldn't have stepped out. It was little digs meant to belittle me here and there, but then he'd always apologize."

"If you don't mind me asking, how did he get almost half the business in the settlement and not alimony?"

"It was considered a material asset. At the time

of the divorce, the only things we had were that and the house, which he bought me out of." The longer she stood there by the dry dock next to the damaged catamaran, the hotter the blood in her veins became. It flowed through her body like the lava coming out of the volcano.

"Let's get back to this charter," Hale said. "I know we've gone over this, but I want to clarify some things. The guests were friends of Vernon's?"

"I don't know if they were friends or not. Vernon told me that Frank was a business associate. An important one. Something about trying to close a deal. Vernon was adamant that I personally take the charter out, even though this boat was scheduled for service this week."

"This is what I'm not understanding. Vernon has nothing to do with the day-to-day operations, right?"

"Generally, no. But he does this sometimes. He'll book something for someone he knows, overriding me, exerting his power as co-owner. If I can accommodate the customer, I'll do it. However, oftentimes I can't, and it causes problems. Once, Vernon went behind my back and contracted a captain and crew from another company to take out one of my boats for a three-day charter after I told him we couldn't do it."

"You've never hired outside your own employees?"

"I'll contract other captains or crew. All my chefs come from a service company. But I go through certain channels to do it. I don't bring anyone aboard I don't know. That particular instance, I had an early scuba run and when I returned, the boat was gone."

"In this situation, what was the deciding factor to allow the charter to go, even though the boat needed service?"

"Vernon told me if his deal with Frank went through, he'd sell me his half of Driftwood Tours for half the market value." She swiped at her cheeks. The one thing she hated more than crying, was doing it in front of people. "I want that man out of my life. That boat." She jerked her finger over her shoulder. "Is only two years old. It was basic service. I'm anal about shit like that. Waiting a week shouldn't be an issue because I'm so meticulous in how I care for my boats. I have the service records to prove it."

"Ma'am, I can say with a fair amount of confidence that this wasn't an accident." He folded his arms. "Who's at fault? That I don't know yet."

Which meant she was a potential suspect. As was everyone who worked for her.

But so was Vernon.

That man was a lot of things, but why would he do this? He'd never raised his hand to anyone that she'd ever seen. He could be mean with his words, but he wasn't violent.

"I think I have all that I need for now," Hale said. "Will you be heading back to the other side of the island?"

"Yes. That's the plan."

"All right. Please don't leave the area. I understand you have a business to run, but if you need to go out on a charter, I need to know about it."

"I'm happy to send you my schedule," she said.

"That would be most helpful." Hale took the sunglasses perched on the top of his head and lowered them over his eyes. "I'll be in touch."

"Thank you." She stood there, frozen in time, watching Hale stroll toward his dark sedan.

"Hey." Remi stepped from the maintenance shed. "That looked intense."

"It was." She folded the document and tucked it in her back pocket.

"Did he mention any suspects? Have any idea who did this? Because I can think of only one person who has it out for you." Remi tilted his head and pursed his lips.

"Yeah, we all know Vernon and I don't like each other much and we fight like motherfuckers. He's a lot of things. A liar. A cheat. A scam artist. But why the hell would he try to blow up a boat with a client he's trying to do business with?"

"Because that would get you out of his life." Remi arched a brow.

She didn't need to be reminded of that.

"Let me call Mano. He'll be able to find out what kind of *deal* Vernon was working on with Frank. That might give us some insight."

"All right. But make sure Mano gives us the friends and family deal. I always give him a discount when he comes for a charter."

"Come on. Knowing him, he'll do it for free."

"That's what I'm afraid of."

Remi laughed. "Let's head home."

"I need to call Waylen and let him know what's going on." She pulled out her cell and tapped the screen, pulling up his contact info.

It went straight to voicemail.

She didn't want to give him the details over the phone.

"Hey, it's me. I've got some news from the investigator. Give me a call when you can. Thanks." She tucked her cell in her back pocket. "Let's roll."

"So, you and Waylen, back in the saddle again. I have to say that warms my heart. The two of you were always a great couple." Remi tossed his arm over her shoulders. He was a big guy at six foot three. He had to be close to two hundred and eighty pounds. He was as wide as a pickup with a personality to match.

"I'm not sure I'd call us a couple. However, I

will say it's been damn good to see him again. He's different but the same, if that makes any sense."

"He's just older. More mature. Kind of a softer, gentler version of his younger self, and his eyes lit up like the best starry night when he climbed up on the boat. It wasn't shock. It was like everything he'd been missing in his life showed up."

"Oh my God. You're a cornball."

"I speak the truth," he said, giving her a hip check. "And you've got a little grin every time you speak of him."

"I absolutely do not." Heat rose to her cheeks like she was a schoolgirl. Ever since Waylen left, Remi and his then-girlfriend, now wife, Akela, had become the two people she trusted the most with her vulnerabilities. Her emotions. Her tears. She could tell them anything and not fear being judged. "Okay, fine. Maybe a little. But he's not here indefinitely. He has a return ticket to the mainland. I'm not going to set myself up to be hurt."

"The two of you being in the same space and not allowing your love to bloom is a recipe for heartbreak for both of you."

"It's twenty-three years of complications."

"That may be true. But you're still in love with the man and don't you dare try to tell me otherwise."

She leaned into Remi's strong frame as they

crossed the parking lot. "The problem is I never stopped."

Waylen leaned back in his chair, eyeing the stage. Ohana's wasn't just any tiki bar. It was *the* place to be. The fact it was for sale had Waylen's mind spinning with possibilities.

Crazy ideas.

But he wasn't the only one who had thought how cool it would be to own a bar or move to Big Island.

However, right now, it was simple chatter. A big idea. A concept. Nothing more. Nothing less.

The waitress brought over two pitchers and a tray of appetizers.

"I think I can speak for everyone that staying a little longer and being on call in case the Brotherhood Protectors need us is no sweat off our backs." Raider raised his frosty mug. "Hawk is about as good as they come."

"Here, here." Harlan clanked his glass. "I could get used to this life."

"What? You're not going to start listing out all the negotiating employment points?" Lane asked with a chuckle.

"We haven't even opened that can of worms

yet." Harlan snagged an onion ring. "But when we do, trust me, I'll have something to say."

"You always do," Kian said. "It's what we love about you." He slapped Harlan on the back. "See any hot chicks you want to hit on for a one-nighter?"

"I seriously don't understand why you bother." Harlan shook his head. "That gets real old, real fast."

"Not for us." Waylen reached across the table and placed a few wings on his plate, doing his best to put that damn piano out of his line of sight. But the fucking thing taunted him, begging him to sit down on the bench and run his fingers across the keys. "We enjoy watching you get indignant about it."

"That's a mighty big word, even for you." Harlan waved his fried treat. "How's your friend Presley doing?"

"Freaked out, and I don't blame her." Waylen had wanted to get in his rental and drive back to the marina the second he'd learned an intentional cut to the line had caused the gas leak. The idea that anyone wanted to hurt Presley made him want to put his fist through the wall.

Better yet, smack-dab in the middle of her asshole ex-husband's face.

Based on everything he'd learned, it had to be him. But Hawk needed him to do some high-tech computer work in the morning regarding a different problem. He couldn't say no. Not if he and his team wanted to discuss working for this outfit.

Remi had promised to watch over Presley until Waylen could get there sometime tomorrow.

Mano had gotten a lock on Vernon.

The bases were covered.

He trusted Mano and Remi as much as he did the four men he currently sat with.

"Have you spoken to the investigator?" Lane asked.

Waylen nodded. "A guy by the name of Hale Pau. He knows Hawk. Respects him and the organization. Mentioned they've worked on a case together before. He promised to keep me in the loop if and when he's got something solid, but so far, he has very little but speculation to go on. He can't be sure she was even the target. It could have been anyone on that boat."

"But that's not what you think," Raider said.

"Nope." He rose. "I've got to hit the head." For most of his life, when he was troubled by something, music helped him gather his thoughts so he could make sense of any situation. As a teenager, he didn't hide his abilities. He openly played the piano or the guitar. And he sang. It was a passion he shared with his father. That and fishing.

He continued when he moved to Maryland, but it didn't feel the same.

His father had died.

And he no longer had Presley at his side.

So, when he entered the Naval Academy, he gave it up, except for when he was all alone or with his mother. That was hard for those four years. But because he always lived alone—except for his short marriage—he could sing and play to his heart's content.

He strolled by the stage. The damn piano might as well have had fucking fingers, reaching out and grabbing him by the heart and yanking him right up on that wooden platform. He studied it for a moment. It was old and weathered but playable. Tapping a finger on one of the keys, he ignored Raider yelling across the bar, asking him what the hell he was doing.

The last time he sang in public had been on Big Island.

At his father's funeral.

It was a bittersweet memory.

"Fuck it." He pulled back the bench and plopped his ass down. Cracking his knuckles, he rolled his neck. "This one's for you, Pops."

He turned the mic on, lowered it to the proper position, sucked in a deep breath, and let his fingers hover over the keyboard.

This wasn't a mainstream song and not everyone loved music from the seventies, but this was one of his father's favorites and he loved to change it up a little.

He pounded the first keystrokes, shifting his gaze to his buddies. He cracked a slight smile. "Whoa," he belted out as he continued playing, leading up to the lyrics of the song.

Kian sat there with his jaw practically in his lap, bug-eyed.

Raider and Harlan were glancing between each other and the stage with shocked expressions.

Lane shook his head and waggled his finger.

When Waylen began singing, his team was on their feet. Every single one of them, including Kian. They whistled, clapped, and even sang along.

Although Waylen tripped them up a little when he sang *Bad, Bad, Waylen Brown* instead Leroy, but that's how he and his dad used to sing it. Made people laugh and his friends were no different.

Waylen ran his fingers across the keyboard, showing off a bit. Chills crawled over his skin from his toes to his neck. The good kind of chills. The ones that oddly made you all warm and tingly.

His buddies went wild.

"You lied to me, you lovable bastard," Lane shouted.

They were the best. He couldn't ask for a better support system than those four. No matter their quirks. Their annoyances. Their flaws. They were the kind of men who showed up when they were at their own rock bottom.

When the song ended, he let out a long breath, dropping his hands in his lap.

Everyone in the bar cheered and begged for another song.

But one was enough. At least for tonight.

He stood and made his way back to the table. A few people stopped him. Thanked him for his service and for the song.

"My God. What other talents are you hiding from us?" Harlan slapped him on the back. "That was amazing. I had no idea you could do that."

"Thanks, man." He pulled back his chair, snagged his beer, and chugged. While he truly loved playing and singing, he loathed being the center of attention.

"It was cool that you changed the name from Leroy to Waylen. But did I hear you toss in a Presley?" Harlan laughed.

"Back in the day that's how I always sang it, so old habits die hard, I guess." Waylen shrugged.

"Don't sing, my ass." Lane leaned across the table and gave him a little punch in the shoulder. "I'm a little in awe of you right now."

"Don't be. It's not that big of a deal. I was just fooling around. It wasn't that good."

"Are you kidding? You could go on one of those singing shows and be a star," Raider said. "I'm not busting your balls either. You're seriously that good. Why have you never told us you could play the piano or sing like that?"

"Yeah. I'm wondering that myself." Kian folded his arms over his chest. He had that tight look on his face that indicated he was a little hurt. Kian was the kind of man who could be seriously misunderstood. He had this rough, tough exterior. But, deep down, he was about as sensitive as they came. He didn't often show it, but when it came to this group, when he did, it came out sideways. "It's weird that you kept that in the vault."

"It was something I did with my dad. He was a great singer. And a songwriter. It was a passion of his and he passed it down to me. But after he died, it seemed all wrong and I just stopped. Being back here and having his memories flood my brain, I wanted to pay a little homage to the old man."

"That's damn fucking sweet." Kian squeezed his shoulder. "But you better not be keeping more secrets. It will break my heart."

"Sometimes you're like a toddler who didn't get his way." Raider shook his head.

"Don't worry. I think that might be the last one." Waylen's cell vibrated in his back pocket. He pulled it out.

"It's Presley. I better take it." He raced toward the parking lot. "Hey, babe. Everything okay?"

"No. It's not," she said with a shaky voice.

He could tell she'd been crying and Presley didn't cry. At least not openly. She had a weird ability to control it better than most.

"What's wrong?" He stopped dead in his tracks. His heart sank to his heels.

She hiccupped. "Someone broke into the Driftwood Tours office. They ransacked it. Went through all my files. I can't tell if they took anything. But they didn't stop there." She spoke so fast he couldn't get a word in if he tried. "Whoever it was decided to go upstairs to the apartment and took my personal laptop." A loud gasp followed by a few sobs filled his ears. "And Waylen is missing."

"No, I'm not."

"Not you. My cat. They left the door open and he got out. He's not an outdoor cat. Akela had been taking care of him for me." More gasps.

"Babe. I need you to take a few deep breaths. Can you do that?"

Silence for a few seconds.

"Presley, is Remi with you?"

"Yes," she whispered.

"And the police?"

"Still here along with Investigator Hale."

"Are they thinking this is tied to the gas leak?" He rubbed the back of his neck.

"They certainly aren't ruling that out." She let out an audible sigh.

"Make sure Remi stays with you. I've got to

make a phone call, but I'll be there as soon as I can. Tell Hale to call me after he wraps up and get all the names and numbers of the police officers. I want to talk with them."

"Okay. But are you sure you can break away? I thought you—"

"Babe. I'm not going let you go through this alone. I'm leaving here within the next twenty minutes. I'll call you from the road."

"All right. Thank you."

"Anything for my Cilla," he said.

"You can't ever call me that again."

"Why not?"

"Do you know what Elvis Presley's father's name was?"

"Vernon," he whispered. "I see your point and I promise I'll find a new nickname for you."

"Don't want one," she said. "I've got to go."

"Stay safe. I'll see you soon." He ended the call and quickly brought up Hawk's number. He answered on the first ring. "Hey, Hawk. It's Waylen."

"What's up?"

"I've got a situation with Presley Miles. Her place was robbed and ransacked and I have reason to believe it has to do with what happened to her boat. I hope you'll understand if I skip out tonight to help her sort through what's happening. I believe she was the target—"

"Waylen. Slow down," Hawk said. "And my answer is you have the full backing of the Brotherhood Protectors."

"Thank you. I appreciate it."

"I'd still like your help. I understand your IT skills are extensive. So, I'll send you the file. You can work on it remotely. It's not a high priority—at least not right now. In the meantime, do you need backup? Because you do have your team or anyone else I have available at your disposal."

"I don't believe so. The police are still with Presley. But if I do, I'd of course like to be able to call on my buddies."

"Fair enough. Keep me posted daily."

"Will do." The phone went dead.

Now it was time to tell the team before packing an overnight bag. Whatever he couldn't stuff in his rucksack in five minutes, he'd buy along the way. He didn't need much.

All he really needed was to protect Presley.

He couldn't let anything happen. He cared for her too much. More than he'd allowed himself to admit over the years.

His mother was right.

His love for her had never faded.

8

*W*aylen slipped from behind the steering wheel of his rental. He wasn't used to having emotions cloud his usually clear head when it came to what he considered a job.

But Presley wasn't an assignment. Even if the Brotherhood Protectors considered her that, she was a woman he cared for and that muddied the waters in ways he had no idea how to compartmentalize.

The cops had left. So had Hale. Waylen had spoken to him twenty minutes ago and while he agreed the two incidents were most likely related, he wasn't jumping to conclusions.

That pissed Waylen right the fuck off. It didn't matter that Waylen understood the man had a job to do and part of that was to look at every angle. Every aspect. If Waylen were in his shoes, he wouldn't be putting his personal spin on it in front of anyone except those he worked closely with.

Meow. Meow. Meeeeooooow.

Waylen paused, craning his ear. The sound was so soft and muffled he wasn't sure he'd even heard it.

Meeeeoooooowwwwww.

Where the hell did that come from? He spun around but didn't see any cat.

He lifted his cell and turned on his flashlight. He looked under his car. Under Presley's vehicle. "Where are you, kitty?" He checked under the stairs that led to the upstairs apartment.

Nothing.

He strolled toward the marina gate. The closer he got to the dumpster, the louder the meowing got. He lifted the lid. "Oh, you poor thing." Reaching his hand inside, he grabbed the scared, dirty, smelly cat. "You're a big boy. Or girl." The cat wore a collar. Waylen fiddled with the tag.

"Waylen." He chuckled as the cat, shaking in his arms, snuggled into his chest. "I got you. Let's go up and see your mommy. She's going to be so relieved you're okay." He scratched the cat's head as he climbed the steps to the upstairs apartment. He couldn't believe this was where she lived. Her parents used to rent it to deckhands, mechanics, or other people who worked for them and needed cheap rent for the short term until they could afford a place in town.

He tapped on the door.

"Who's there?" Remi's voice boomed through the wood barrier.

"It's Waylen. Open up."

"How was the... you found Waylen." Remi glanced over his shoulder.

Presley bolted off the couch and took the four steps to the door. "My cat!" She grabbed the kitty from Waylen's arms. "My little Waylen." She hugged and kissed him before scrunching her nose. "Oh my God. What is that smell? Where have you been?"

"Sadly, I found him in the dumpster." Waylen put his hands on his hips. He stared at Presley as she continued to show affection for her cat. Named Waylen.

And not the man named Waylen.

Being jealous of a cat was about the dumbest fucking thing ever.

"Oh, you poor baby. Let's go get you cleaned up." She kissed the cat's nose as she turned toward the bathroom. Glancing over her shoulder, she smiled weakly. "Thank you. Not just for finding my cat. But for coming."

"Of course." He nodded.

"I haven't seen her like this since you moved to Maryland," Remi said. "Do you want a drink?"

"Does she have anything stiffer than a beer?"

"It's Presley. Of course she does." Remi laughed.

"This place hasn't changed much." He scanned the room.

The same surfboard bed was pushed up against the west wall, but with a different comforter, which made him chuckle because the anchor in the middle of it was so Presley.

A couch faced the east, where a small television was hung on the wall.

On the south wall was the kitchen and tiny island. Next to that, the door to the bathroom.

Other than a small closet, that's all there was and this is what Presley called home.

Well, he'd lived in worse over the years.

Remi handed him a short glass of scotch on the rocks.

"Jesus. I remember the first time I tried this stuff."

"It was the night before you left."

Waylen laughed. "Not the first time I got drunk, but I was so hungover on that plane. I got sick like ten times. My mom wanted to be pissed, but she couldn't. She still carries some guilt for moving me."

"We missed you, man." Remi clanked his glass against Waylen's. "Especially Presley. And that display with the cat, well, you should know she was worried that Vernon killed the damn thing."

"That might have been what he was trying to do by putting the poor thing in the garbage. If it wasn't, it certainly sent a message about how he feels about the cute little bugger." Waylen took a sip of the brown liquid. It warmed his belly. Over the years, he'd developed a taste for the liquor, but it always reminded him of the friends he'd left behind.

"Have you talked to Mano? I thought he was tailing Vernon."

"He has been. Unfortunately, Vernon parked his vehicle in the garage, and then four other cars came. Looked like he was having a party. At the time of the break-in, two cars had left, but Mano said it didn't appear Vernon had."

"Doesn't mean he didn't switch clothes or something with one of his guests or hired someone to do his dirty work."

"That's what Mano thinks." Waylen planted his ass on the stool. "Hale promised to call me after questioning Vernon, but it gives him a built-in alibi."

"That man is a fucking asshole. I swear to God, he targeted Presley from the get-go."

"I might not have seen her since she was seventeen, but she's not the kind of person to fall for a man's charm. I mean, she didn't fall for Mano, and he tried. I thought I would have to fight him to get him to back off."

"Your memory is way off when it comes to

Mano." Remi leaned against the counter. "But Vernon came into her life at a strange time. Coming home after college was hard. Everything reminded her of you and she didn't know what she wanted to do with her life. Some of us were getting married or moving away. When she wasn't working for her parents, she worked on yachts as a deckhand, bouncing between the islands. After a while, her mom started to struggle, but no one knew what was wrong with her, and you know Presley. She was always fiercely protective and insanely close with her folks."

"I didn't know her mom was sick for that long."

"It was a gradual thing and she hated doctors. It wasn't until after Presley married Vernon that she got her mom to get all the tests the docs wanted her to have, but by then it was too late. The cancer was everywhere. There was no hope."

"What was so special about this Vernon asshole that she fell that hard and fast? Because she hates him now and I don't mean like most exes do. She passionately loathes the man."

"In the beginning, on the outside, he treated her like a princess. He had a good job, was making money, and helped out with the family business. It wasn't until the miscarriage that his true colors came out." He jerked his thumb over his shoulder. "Naming the cat was a *fuck you* to Vernon. Only he had no idea for a year or two who Waylen was."

"I can't imagine what happened when he found out she named her cat and her boat after me."

"They got into a huge fight and not the normal yelling. She laid into him and you know how she gets. She nailed him with every transgression. She didn't hold anything back."

"That woman can fight dirty." Waylen almost wished he'd been a fly on the wall for that conversation. In all the years he and Presley had been friends, then boyfriend and girlfriend, they'd had their share of arguments. Some were typical and some weren't pretty. She could hit below the belt when she felt backed into a corner. She was a fiery, feisty woman. Passionate. Loving. But one didn't dare piss her off. "But the one thing I know for sure is she gives people she cares about many chances before she comes out swinging. He had to have done something obnoxious for her to name a cat after me."

"That's a story for her to tell," Remi said. "I've already given you too much as it is. She hates it when people gossip about her business." He raised his glass, downing the last few drops. "I need to get home to my wife and kid."

"I'd really love to meet your family and see Akela again." Waylen shook his head. "I can't believe you and she are married. I always knew you liked her, but you had big dreams of leaving and she was never going to follow you."

"No, she wasn't. But when I came back, I knew there wasn't another woman on this earth for me." Remi smiled. "When I told her you were back in town, it brought tears to her eyes. She'd love to cook you a nice Hawaiian meal when all this calms down."

"Consider me there." He stretched out his arm.

Remi gripped his hand. "Hale said the cops will be patrolling the area."

"Mano's got a friend hanging around too. I'll call my team in if necessary."

"I know she's in good hands." Remi rinsed out his glass and placed it in the tiny dishwasher. He'd always been the kind of guy to do stuff like that. "I've got a snorkel charter in the morning, so I'll check on you both then."

Waylen stared into his drink. The ice had melted a tad. He twirled it before bringing it to his lips and sipping. A million things ran through his brain. He'd left a piece of himself on this island. He'd given Presley his heart.

When he left Big Island, he never believed it would end. But the more he poured himself into his studies at the Naval Academy, the more he understood Presley and her letters. And she was right. They both needed to focus on their education.

He did his best to put her out of his mind and forge forward.

He believed he'd succeeded. But in reality, she

was etched into his soul. Elena was right. Presley was a ghost in their marriage. However, it was more than that. He spent twenty-three years living a life—that he was born to navigate—all so he could return to this place.

Because this was where he belonged.

This was home.

"You're a weird kitty." Presley poured more water on Waylen, rising off the cat-friendly soup. "You're not supposed to like baths."

Meow. Waylen rubbed his head against her hand.

"I love you too." She leaned over and kissed his nose. "I'm sorry that mean man hurt you. I won't ever let him near you again."

It had to be Vernon. No one else hated her this much, but she didn't understand why. When they divorced, he'd done a complete flip. He acted as if he wanted to stay married. He told the judge he wanted to go to therapy but that she had refused.

Lie. It was the other way around.

He went on about how he'd started dissolving his business so they could work together at Drift-wood Tours.

Another lie. She didn't know what the hell was going on with his job or why he suddenly had no money. But she knew he'd taken money from Driftwood Tours and depleted their bank accounts.

His explanation for that was that, against his better judgment, he'd allowed her to make questionable business decisions, which put the family business at risk.

Asshole.

The fucker was a damn good con artist and she'd been one of his greatest conquests.

Tears burned the corners of her eyes.

Meow. Her cat placed his paws on the side of the tub and nuzzled his face in her neck.

"You're a sweet boy, Way-Way. And that's what we'll have to call you because Waylen, the man, has returned. He's the one who saved you. He saved me too." She snagged a towel and wrapped up Way-Way, snuggling him close and rubbing his fur. She opened the door and set the cat on the floor. He danced between her legs before darting off to do the same to Waylen. "He likes you."

"I like him too." Waylen reached down and scratched Way-Way's head. "How are you holding up?"

Fuck. Here came the waterworks. Crying didn't make her weak, but it sure as hell made her feel that way. Her father had always told her that there was a time and place for her tears, and she needed to learn to control her emotions. She was a woman working in a male-dominated industry, and they were going to try to beat her down at every turn. If she showed them they could push her buttons, she wouldn't last five seconds.

"Hey. Come here." Waylen stretched out his arms.

She caved, diving into them, gripping his strong frame with all her might.

He was safe. He wasn't going to belittle her or tell her to pack up and go home. No. He'd let her cry it out and then tell her to fight like hell.

"I'm here. I got you." He kissed her temple.

"I fucking hate this."

"I know," he whispered, lifting her off the floor. He carried her to the bed and climbed onto the mattress, keeping her between his legs with her head on his chest. "If I were in your shoes, I'd be bawling like a baby."

"No. You'd punch a wall."

"That too." He laughed.

She sucked in a deep breath, letting it out slowly. "Vernon has done a lot of shitty things. He's lied to me and to my parents. He used me. He's gotten into some shady things. Cheated on me, although that just gave me the push I needed to divorce his sorry ass. But this is over the top, even for him."

"I'm not sure it is."

She jerked her head. "What does that mean? You've never even met him. You only know the crappy stuff I've told you. Or maybe what Remi's put in your head." She covered Waylen's mouth. "Trust me, I'm not defending Vernon. He's a prick. But I can't wrap my brain around why he'd try to blow up my boat with me, Remi, or his business associate on it."

"Hale told me that no one on that boat knows anything about a business deal, including Frank's wife."

"That doesn't mean jack shit. If Frank's into something shady, then why would they admit to anything?"

"You're right about that, and Hale is looking into it, but this break-in points to you being the target. That means whoever did these things is after you."

She shivered.

He held her tighter.

"Don't get mad. But I did some poking around in Vernon's financials."

"You did what?" She bolted to a sitting position and brushed her hair from her face. "As in, you illegally hacked into his bank records? You could get into some serious trouble for that."

Waylen shrugged. "Part of my job in the military was cyber intelligence. I got paid to do some illegal shit." He smiled.

She smacked his shoulder. "I can't believe I'm going to ask this, but what did you find out?"

"Yeah. You're not going to like this." He took

her hand. "All of this is conjecture. I have no proof and because I am skirting half a dozen laws, I couldn't go too deep. But I'm wondering if Vernon wasn't possibly using your boats to do some smuggling of something."

"You've got to be kidding me." She cocked her head. "He tried to reroute the boats to give his so-called VIP clients a *wow* experience. But it wasn't that far off the beaten path."

"It doesn't matter. All it takes is a meet-and-greet with one boat where puddle pirates or other authorities aren't generally looking to do a trade."

The blood in her veins turned ice-cold. "I'm going to fucking go off on that man if he put me or any of my crew in—"

Waylen pressed his finger over her lips. "Babe, I'm making a guess based on very little information, and I don't need you going off half-cocked, landing yourself in jail for doing something stupid."

"I'm so angry I could scream."

"Well, maybe I should keep the rest of what I found to myself."

She poked his biceps. "Don't you dare."

He held up his hands. "I'm not exactly sure what he's into, but it appears the businesses he's gotten involved with are fronts to launder money and that he might have been either setting this place up to do that, or he was, until you got in the way by divorcing him and taking over the books again."

"I always had one hand on the books. He just kept finding ways to stop me." She let out a sigh.

"How?"

"Well, when we first got married, he acted like he wanted to be part of it, but more in a supportive role. He learned the business, but he still worked outside of Driftwood Tours. He kept telling me to relax and take time for myself. He thought I worked too much and it was interfering with me getting pregnant. After the miscarriage, once he apologized for blaming me for it, he begged me to take time off so I could put it behind me and we could try again. Then it was about helping my mom. Or taking the load off after she died. Or my dad died. There was always a reason for me to back off and for him to take over. He's so fucking good with words and making you feel like you're the problem."

"I know people like him."

"I should have seen what a snake he was before I married the douchebag."

Waylen leaned in, kissing her tenderly. "People like him are masters at finding someone's weakness and exploiting it. One of your biggest flaws is you tend to take the burdens of the world on your shoulders. You put other people's needs before your own. Even when I first met you and we were like ten, you would take care of all your friends before you'd do a single thing for yourself." He placed his hand in the center of her chest. "You have the biggest heart of anyone I've ever met. And that's an awesome thing to have. But when you combine that with your uncanny ability to believe everything is your fault..." He cocked a brow. "Like the day my father died."

"I still feel bad about that."

"Babe. Me staying a little longer with you wasn't going to save him."

"We don't—"

He pressed his finger over her lips. "Yeah. We do. He didn't have just any heart attack. It was the widow-maker. Not only that, but the autopsy showed the blockage was at ninety-nine percent. His heart just stopped. The doctors told us that even if we'd seen him drop, the likelihood they could have saved him was slim."

"But there could have been a chance. If only I hadn't asked you to stay."

Waylen let out an audible sigh, running a hand over his face. "I've thought long and hard about that day for years. I blamed myself, and you, better than anyone, know that. I was more upset that he died alone. That my mom had to go on without him. But I never once blamed you. I decided to stay and we had no way of knowing. However, if I had held you responsible, you're the kind of woman who would have taken that and ran with it. If I hadn't been able to comprehend what happened to my dad, you'd be holding on to that as fact, instead of simply feeling bad. Do you see my point?"

"Kind of," she admitted. It wasn't the first time she'd heard that. Akela had been telling her that for years.

"We can all be exploited," Waylen said.

"I bet you can't."

"You'd lose that bet," he said. "I was captured and tortured once."

"Is that what the scars are from on your back?"

He nodded. "It took them three days to break me. But they did."

"How?"

"They found one of my biggest weak spots. My mother." He pursed his lips. "And how she'd feel about her son being sent home in a body bag. That's all it took. Lucky for me, before I gave them everything, my team busted through the door and saved me. But even a badass Navy SEAL can be exploited. It might take someone a little longer, but it happens."

"I'm sorry that happened to you."

"I lived to tell the tale and went home and kissed my mama. That's all that matters."

She cupped his face. "You're a good man, Waylen."

"'Cause a good woman raised me."

"My God, once a mama's boy, always a mama's

boy. And you're still the corniest guy I know." She dropped her hands to her sides.

"Just a little humor because there are a few things we still need to talk about before we get naked under these sheets." He waggled his brows.

"You think you're getting laid?"

"You think I'm not?"

"You're insufferable." She shook her head, laughing. "What else is on your mind?"

"Do you have a will?"

"That's a weird-ass question." She narrowed her stare. "But yes."

"Where is it?"

"There's a copy of it with my attorney and one here. Why?"

"Have you checked to see if it's still here?"

Her lips went numb. Her face tingled. She jumped off the bed, nearly knocking the cat over.

Way-Way snarled, running out of the way.

Presley raced to the closet and opened the door. She rummaged through the accordion file case where she kept a few personal documents. Her heart dropped before lurching to her throat. She stood, still holding the case as she stepped into the room. "It's gone."

"Anything else missing?" He sat cross-legged with a grim expression.

She shook her head. "Why would he take that?"

"Before I answer that, who gets your half of Driftwood Tours if you were to die tomorrow?"

"That's fucking morbid," she muttered, climbing back on the bed.

"Just answer the question."

"Mano."

"Are you kidding me? Why the hell did you ask him?" He raked his fingers through his hair. "Why not Remi?"

"Because he doesn't want to deal with Vernon. Trust me, I asked him."

"Okay. That's fair. But Mano? The man had a thing for you when we were kids and he probably still does."

"Are you jealous?"

Waylen tapped his finger to his chest. "Me. No. Never. Not of hunky, sexy, rich man Mano who used to buy my girlfriend flowers, chocolates, and offer to take her for rides in all his fancy toys."

She ran her finger along the side of his face and across his lower lip. "Mano was not in love with me back then. And he's certainly not in love with me now. He was one of your best friends growing up. He's like a big goofy brother and you know that. But he did kind of like fucking with you when it came to me."

"And you enjoyed going along with it."

"Only because you knew I was your girl."

Waylen smiled. "That is a true statement."

"But Mano doesn't like Vernon. Not one fucking bit."

"He did make that perfectly clear," Waylen said. "Do you know who gets Vernon's half if he dies?"

"Yeah, me," Presley said. "In our divorce settlement, because it was a family business, I was able to negotiate that little piece. The judge made it clear that I have to be left Driftwood Tours."

"I'm glad for that," Waylen said. "By chance, did you give Mano a copy of your will?"

"No."

"All right. First thing in the morning, we need to call your lawyer and get a new copy. I'll work a little of my IT magic and see if I can find out if Vernon has made a fake one on your behalf."

"Jesus, you really think he's trying to kill me?"

"I don't know, but I'm not going to sit around and wait for him or anyone else to try to hurt you again. He's going to have to come through me. Besides, I care too much and I'm not going to lose this chance to get to know you again."

"That's both a little Neanderthalish and sweet at the same time."

"I do still care very much about you. No matter where I've been in the world or what I've been doing, that's a fact that has never changed."

She pushed him back and straddled his hips. Her pulse raged. "That same holds true for me."

He flipped her on her back and kissed her hard.

The kiss was a whirlwind of passion and longing, years of separation melting away instantly. As their bodies pressed together, the weight of their shared history hung heavy in the air. It was a dance they knew well, the push and pull of desire and restraint, a familiar rhythm that neither could resist. In that moment, all doubts and fears vanished, leaving only the raw vulnerability of two souls laid bare before each other once more. And as their bodies entwined, they found solace in the familiarity of each other's touch, knowing that no matter what challenges lay ahead, they would face them together.

Her hands sought out familiar paths, tracing scars and curves that time had etched into his body.

The room filled with the echo of whispered promises and the scent of rekindled desires. Each touch was like a stolen memory as she surrendered to the pull of their undeniable connection, their bodies moving in perfect harmony as if no time had passed at all.

Outside, she knew danger lurked in the background, waiting to pounce. But within those walls, time stood still, a sanctuary where past and present converged in a symphony of passion and love that had weathered every storm. As she clung to both their past love and their present need, she worried that this reunion could still be a fleeting moment instead of a chance to rewrite the story that fate had once torn apart.

He covered their bodies with the blanket, wrapping his arms around her and kissing her shoulder. "We did it again," he whispered.

"No shit, Sherlock."

"Not that." He chuckled. "I meant we were reckless again."

She closed her eyes. There was a part of her that wasn't worried. That wasn't scared.

But she should be utterly terrified for so many reasons.

"It's not like us to be like that. We never once went without when we were kids, and that's when people make idiot mistakes."

9

Waylen slipped from the bed as carefully and quietly as he could. He didn't want to disturb Presley. She needed her sleep. But he had to contend with the damn cat that decided he liked to snuggle between Waylen and Presley and he wasn't going to be moved. Every time Waylen tried, his namesake came right back.

After four attempts to find the cat a suitable spot on the bed that wasn't wedged between him and Presley, Waylen gave up.

He hiked up his jeans and pulled his shirt over his head. The cat purred and stretched at the edge of the bed before jumping to the ground and racing toward Waylen so the silly kitty could dance around his legs and rub up against them. Waylen bent over, lifting the cute little bugger up, scratching his head. "I'm gonna go get some coffee and breakfast sandwiches. I'll be right back," he whispered, wiggling his feet into his shoes. Gently, he set the cat on the mattress and slipped out the door.

Raking his fingers through his hair, he stared out into the harbor. He sucked in a deep breath, enjoying the salty air. He'd been a lucky man most of his life. Sure, he'd experienced death, heartache, torture, divorce, among other things. But overall, he had his health. A loving mother. Great friends. The perfect career. He'd even experienced the best kind of love with Presley.

His heart tightened. There was always that chance his team didn't want to stay. Or they didn't go after the job with the Brotherhood Protectors. Or if they did, Hank Patterson, the head of the entire organization, sent Waylen and the boys somewhere else.

The plan had always been to retire together and continue on as a team. They were all on board.

Waylen's heart fractured. He wanted to work with his brothers. That meant the world to him.

But he wanted to stay on Big Island and find out if this exciting twist of fate had been what Father Time had in store for him all along. He didn't know how to reconcile that conflict in his mind.

Or his soul.

"Yo, Waylen. What's uuuupppp?"

He leaned over the railing and tried not to smile. "Hey. If it isn't Mr. Popular." In middle school, they

149

weren't friends because Waylen only saw Mano as the cool kid.

Mano hated it because the kids only liked him because he was rich. It had taken Mano a few years to learn that tough lesson, but once he did, he had developed a sixth sense about who wanted to hang with him because they wanted to see his parents' mansion, go for a ride in one of the family's fancy vehicles, or go on the yacht, or better yet, the private helicopter.

Waylen and Mano had bonded over being used by their peers for things they couldn't control— Waylen for being smart, Mano for being born into a rich family. They were two young boys who, by all means, shouldn't be friends if you went by the standard social construct of young kids and teenagers. But none of that mattered to them.

"I never thought I'd say this, but it's damn good to have you back on this island." Mano held up a tray of coffee and a bag. "Little Miss Sunshine awake yet?"

Waylen shook his head. "Where's her ex?" He jogged down the steps.

"Hale's talking to him and when he's done, I've got two people posted on his house." Mano handed him a mug of coffee.

"Do you know anything about Hale?"

"Yeah. We've butted heads a few times on some cases I've worked, but at the end of the day, he's a good man. Excellent at his job. He'll do right by Presley."

"That's comforting."

"Hale can be tough. He won't cut corners and he might piss you off. But he's all about justice and he'll work with you. He respects the Brotherhood Protectors and the military," Mano said. "I'm sorry about yesterday. Someone rarely gives me the slip and Vernon's a slippery asshole. He's smarter than he looks. Fucking master manipulator is what he is."

"How well do you know him?"

"Well enough to want to rip his eyes from his head. He didn't like me and Presley hanging out and I didn't want to make things hard for her, even if I didn't believe he was the right man, so I kept my distance but never turned my back. I know people who have crossed paths with Vernon." Mano jerked his head toward the marina. "Let's go sit on that picnic table over there."

"All right." Waylen raised the mug and sniffed before taking a sip of the amazing brew. "Sweet Jesus. You remembered."

"That you're a weirdo and like vanilla and hazelnut in your coffee?" Mano shook his head. "Who drinks that at seventeen?"

"Me." Waylen laughed. He took the bag and reached inside. "Please tell me you got a sandwich with sausage, bacon, double egg, and hot sauce."

"You're so fucking predictable." He pointed to

the apartment. "Just like ending up with Presley. How long did that take? Five seconds."

"Jealous?"

"More like doing a little happy dance inside." Mano climbed up on top of the table. He almost never sat on the bench. "I've watched Presley put on a smile and tell everyone that she was fine. That everything was going to be dandy after you left. She's a strong girl who believed you'd come back together. But that resolve broke as life happened. She did her best to take care of business and her parents, but it was rough for a bit."

"I'm surprised you didn't step in and sweep her off her feet." Waylen found the sandwich he'd been looking for. He opened the wrapper and his taste buds went wild. He lifted the greasy treat and took a big-ass bite. Still the best fucking breakfast in the world.

Mano laughed. "Even if I had feelings for her, which I never did, I would never do that to you. You and Presley have always been family."

"I hate to admit it, but I've missed your ugly face." Waylen's heart swelled. They'd all grown into bigger, better versions of the same stupid teenagers they once were. This felt easy. Like a comfortable old weathered shoe that you'd do anything to keep from having to toss out.

"Damn, man. Such a sentimental sap." Mano patted his chest. "But you know, you never treated me like the other kids did, and I didn't diss you just because you were a nerd—and you, my friend, drove the nerd bus." Mano shook his head. "Why kids think being smart is a flaw. I was forgiven that talent because my family had money. But it didn't mean anyone liked me for who I was. They only wanted to be my friend because I could take everyone out for pizza and soda after school. I never understood why those who sat at the popular table never softened up to you," Mano said. "You're good people. The best."

"I can't say I've ever spent much time thinking about it."

"Living on this island, dealing with some of the same people, I do," Mano said. "For me, it's either all the little assholes we used to know want to impress me now, show me up, or still want to hang with me to be cool. Like hey, I went to high school with you, dude. I'm too old for that shit."

"Try going to a bar with a flattop haircut in a Navy town. The first question out of some chick's mouth was almost always *are you a SEAL*. I answered no. They moved on, looking for their catch of the day. Most men gave the same response as I did. SEALs are in general a humble lot, but there was always one or two who wanted to get laid and went for it, hoping crazy eyes didn't come out. I get it. Some people could never see past the money. But kids gave you a chance. They got to know you despite what they first saw. However, they saw me solely as the geek who was two or three grades ahead of them in most subjects. I understand how intimidating that can be, especially when I didn't do anything to hide it and the teachers always called me out on it."

"And the only reason you didn't graduate early was because of Presley." Mano laughed.

"Actually, that's false." Waylen wiped his fingers on the napkin. "The earliest I could attend the Naval Academy was seventeen. Same with joining the Navy. Leaving high school even a year early didn't make sense." He shrugged. "So, I was the asshole who took every advanced course our school had to offer, along with a few courses that weren't typical so that I wasn't completely bored."

"You were a walking font of useless information —until someone like me needed it, like when I asked you to help me hack into a few things." Mano leaned forward. "I learned a lot of tricks from you, my friend, which is one of the reasons I decided to make a personal visit this morning."

"Should I go get Sleeping Beauty?"

"You can tell her at your leisure." Mano pushed his food to the side. "I did some looking into Frank."

"Hale told me that Frank's had some issues with the law over the years, but they haven't been able to get anything on him since he moved to Big Island."

"He came over from the main island about six

years ago. He got in a shit ton of trouble as a kid, but who didn't."

Waylen lifted his hand and pointed to his head. "Me."

Mano chuckled. "However, he ended up doing some time for armed robbery and assault when he was twenty. Since then, he's kept his nose clean. But there are rumors he's involved in drug dealing. Arms dealing. Some other shit. The federal government has looked into his business, but they don't have anything to go on or open an active case file."

"I take it you found something that might push that along?" He polished off the last of his coffee.

"I'm not exactly sure. Forensic accounting was never my strong suit. But I saw some red flags. I figured you could do a deeper dive."

"Anything that ties Frank to Vernon?"

Mano ran his hand over his goatee. "I honestly don't know what I'm looking at. I follow people for a living. I might take a peek at bank records. I know how to flag payoffs, shit like that. But this is way above my pay grade."

"What made you think there was something to it?"

"Large sums of cash deposits and withdrawals with people's names next to the ledger."

Waylen jerked his head. "On a bank statement?"

"No. Personal records. Handwritten."

"Where the fuck did you get those?" Waylen cocked his head.

"I have my methods. Anyway, I took pictures of them and emailed the files to you."

"You could have just called to tell me that."

"I wanted to see your pretty face." He reached out and squeezed his cheek. "Because it is adorable."

"Fuck off." He swatted his hand away.

"There is one other thing," Mano said. "A few people have come and gone from Vernon's place. I'm a small operation. It's me, my girl who runs the front office, and I've got two buddies who do contract work for me. I can only do so much."

"I'll call my team. They can be here in a couple of hours. You tell me what you need help with when it comes to Vernon. We can pool our resources."

"That would be fantastic." Mano stood. "Your team is welcome to stay at my place."

"They can get rooms at—"

Mano held up his hand. "I've got a huge house a mile from here. It has ten bedrooms. Me and my girl, Bella, rattle around in there, getting lost. I won't take no for an answer." He lowered his chin. "And if my parents were still alive, they would insist."

"All right. Thanks, man." Waylen gave his old friend a bro-hug.

"Keep that girl of ours safe."

"You know I will."

"And don't knock her up." Mano had said that same thing a dozen times when they'd been teenagers. It had been a running joke. Not necessarily the funniest one, but Mano and Remi thought it was freaking hilarious.

Waylen glared. "That wasn't funny when we were kids and it's not funny now."

"Oh yes, it is, only you're grown-ass adults, and everyone always thought you'd make some gorgeous kids." Mano slapped him on the shoulder. "Stay in touch." He strolled through the parking lot and around the corner.

Waylen snagged the bag and the second coffee. His heart thumped in his chest like a jackhammer. Being back with Presley had turned his world upside down. He'd spent years pushing her from his mind, and he'd done a decent job of it until his divorce. Since then, she'd been all he could think about the moment things went quiet. There was no confusion about wanting to be with her or his desire for a second chance.

But this damn baby thing and being irresponsible at forty had him questioning his sanity. He should be utterly terrified.

However, after all these years, the thought of that kind of life with Presley was like living the dream. He let out a long sigh. Time to go wake her up.

It was going to be a long day.

"I understand." Presley held her cell to her ear and closed her eyes. This was the third cancellation since the news of the accident broke.

Which wasn't an accident at all.

"Is there any chance we can get a refund on the deposit?" the customer asked.

"I'm sorry. Our policy this late in the process specifically states no refunds. However, I will happily apply it to another date if you wish to rebook. Considering the circumstances, that can be at any time in the future."

"That doesn't help me right now."

"I apologize for the inconvenience. But I do have a business to run and I can assure you that all safety measures are being taken."

"I need to think about this," the customer said. "Can you hold the reservation while I chat with my friends to see what they want to do?"

"Absolutely. And like I said, I'm happy to rebook for any available dates."

"I appreciate that. I'll be in touch."

The line went dead.

Presley set the phone on the counter and groaned. If people kept canceling, this could ruin her business. Part of her wanted to give everyone back their deposits, but if she did that, she'd deplete her bank accounts.

"Hey, babe." Waylen strolled into the office. He leaned over the counter and took her chin with his thumb and forefinger. He kissed her tenderly. "You look like you have the weight of the world on your shoulders."

"It's been a long day."

"Is there anything you must do before closing the office?"

"No." She shook her head.

"My team and Blake are over at Al and Lisa's. Let's go get some dinner."

"I didn't know she was coming." Presley tucked her hair behind her ears. The only person she'd met from the team so far had been Kian, and she was dreading meeting everyone else.

Waylen spoke so highly of them, and they all seemed larger than life. These men were the brothers Waylen never had. His family. She knew he'd do anything for them, including designing his future around them. Being jealous of them and their bond with Waylen was simply insane. They had spent years working in a dangerous environment together.

She was part of his past.

They were his present and future.

"What's going on inside that pretty little head of yours?" Waylen inched around the counter and lifted her out of the chair, pulling her into his arms.

She could be a little honest with Waylen. "The

ripple effect from what happened to Frank and it being on the news isn't helping business."

"I can't imagine it has."

"I'm so angry at Vernon and his lies. I can't believe he told Hale that he never proposed selling me his half and offered to reschedule the charter if the *Waylen* needed service. It's such bullshit and all it serves is to make me look bad. The worst part is I have no witnesses."

"You do have one." He kissed her forehead.

"Him making the reservation doesn't prove anything."

"We're going to nail him and he will end up behind bars. I promise."

She believed Waylen. She really did. Her only worry was at what cost? And to whom?

"Come on. I'm hungry and I bet you haven't eaten since this morning." He cupped her face and stared into her eyes with a loving gaze.

"I don't really feel like socializing."

He cocked his brow. "This isn't only about hanging out. The boys and I need to discuss what we found out today. That directly concerns you and I don't want to leave you out. I know better."

"Yeah, you'd be sleeping on one of the boats if you did that."

He chuckled, curling his fingers through her hand and tugging her toward the door. "You're going to love the guys."

At least she was meeting all of them on her turf and she'd have a girlfriend to hang out with while Waylen and his buddies were tossing around all their inside jokes.

Because that was what Waylen had always been known for.

She leaned against his strong frame as he meandered down the path through the marina and into Al and Lisa's bar and restaurant. It was a quaint dive bar that catered to the tourists. They often had great local bands for live music and at the end of a charter, it was the best place for her customers to spend their last evening in paradise.

The only thing that felt magical in Presley's life right now was the return of Waylen, but even that was tainted.

"Hey, girl." Blake greeted her with a smile and open arms. "How are you holding up?"

"I'm vertical. That says something."

"This guy treating you good?" Blake jerked her chin in the direction of Waylen.

He looped his arm around her shoulders. "Like a princess."

"You better or you'll have to deal with me," Blake said. "We got a table in the back."

"Perfect. Let me go introduce you to the guys." He nudged her through the bar area.

Her pulse hammered in her throat. She hadn't been this nervous since she took her captain's test.

"Hey, guys. This is Presley. You know Kian over there," Waylen said.

Kian smiled and waved from the far end of the table.

Oddly, Blake took a seat between him and another man.

"Next to Blake——"

"Let me guess." Presley had heard story after story about each one of these men. In her soul, she felt as though she were weirdly connected to them. "And I bet I can do it by nickname."

"You told her the stupid dumbass names you blessed us with?" Harlan raised his drink and sipped. "What's wrong with you? Have you not learned anything about keeping certain details to yourself? In this case not for future leverage, but just fucking human decency."

"You didn't have to open your mouth for me to know that your nickname is Sabian, but you're really Harlan," Presley said. "I loved Kevin Spacey as Chris Sabian in the movie *The Negotiator*."

"I'll agree it was a good movie, though not really how things are done and I'm better-looking." Harlan raised his glass.

"I made the mistake of suggesting an action military movie last night and I thought Waylen was going to break the TV because everything was wrong." She rolled her eyes.

"They don't get much right on film," Harlan

said. "But let's see if you can get the rest of the gang right."

"She'll never do it. I mean, you were easy. You gave it away with your rhetoric. But the rest of us? She'll screw it up. No offense, but I doubt you'll be able to blow my mind with that shit." This man sat on the other side of Harlan, and he made an explosion sign with both hands on the side of his head.

Based on that, the average person would guess he was Raider, the explosives expert.

But something told her this was Lane. The whole concept of *he doesn't stay in his lane* made her think that.

She narrowed her stare. "You're Lane. Or as Waylen likes to call you, Tracy."

"Jesus, she's good." Lane took a big swig of his beer.

"So, that leaves you, Raider. Or should I call you Blitz?"

"I much prefer Raider, thank you." He smiled. "But at least my nickname is cool and makes sense."

"I don't know about that. Ancient is one of the proper translations for Kian. I actually asked Waylen if that's the name he gave him."

Every man burst out laughing, except Kian, who muttered, "So not funny."

The waitress came over and took appetizer and more drink orders. She noticed the guys had ordered water or a soda, instead of a second round.

Waylen had leaned over and whispered in her ear that to be safe, they wanted to make sure they all stayed sober.

She appreciated that, but at the same time, it made her nervous as fuck. Hale had mentioned that whatever was going on, the break-in could have been the end of it. That Vernon had stolen whatever it was that he wanted.

Only he had her personal computer. If he hacked into that, he had access to her personal bank accounts. Her email. Her world.

Waylen had changed all her passwords and put some alert system on it so he'd know if someone was poking around. But Vernon was smart and wicked. He'd cross whatever line he needed to get what he wanted.

He used to want Driftwood Tours.

When she fought like hell to keep it, he then made it impossible for her to be soul owner. She always wondered why he chose to be tied to her that way. It wasn't because he loved her, that was for damn sure.

"So, Presley, tell us something we don't know about Waylen," Raider said. "We want to know what he was like when he was that skinny, dorky kid in that picture behind the bar."

"Oh, jeez." She pulled her hair over her shoulder and twisted.

"I'm not much different. Just bigger, stronger,

and better at video games," Waylen said, squeezing her thigh, as if to suggest she not tell a single embarrassing story.

"Did you know he was on the chess team?" Presley said.

Harlan set his drink aggressively on the table. "You don't say."

"I shouldn't be surprised, but damn, I am," Lane said. "But only because in all the rooms we've sat around playing cards and other stupid shit, waiting for something happen, he never once played checkers or chess with anyone."

"That's because I would have beaten all of you in five minutes. It would have bored me to tears," Waylen said. "Now that's enough storytelling for one night."

"Oh, I've got another good one for you." Presley sat up taller and squared her shoulders. In a matter of a half hour, she understood Waylen's bond with his buddies. They were more than friends. More than teammates. They were male soulmates. Each and every single one. She felt that to her core. "The only time he got in trouble at school was when he hacked into the grading system and actually tried to change his A to a B."

"Why the fuck would you do that?" Lane asked. "Didn't you graduate with like a perfect score?"

Waylen shook his head. "Do you know what it's like to be popularly unpopular? Kids only wanted me around if I could help them get a better grade. They wanted to cheat off me. Or have me take their tests. Some did actually want me to tutor them. But outside of that, I was invisible. I thought if I gave myself a normal-ish grade, kids would see me differently."

"Dude, by the time you hit high school, that ship has sailed," Harlan said.

"When he pulled that little stunt, he'd been in the sixth grade. It was how we became good friends. We were in detention together." Presley laughed, shaking her head. "I remember telling my dad about this boy who was so tech-savvy he could hack his way into the school computer system. My father was both mortified and impressed. He wanted me to invite Waylen over to the house. So I did. My dad and Waylen fell in love with each other. It was the biggest bromance I'd ever seen." Presley raised her hand to the ceiling. "Swear to God, those two would sit around playing chess, checkers, cards, talking about politics, and Waylen set up our computer system because my dad lived in the freaking dark ages. He also taught my parents the two-step."

Waylen dropped his head to the table and groaned.

"Wait. What?" Kian said. "Is this another secret? Does Waylen know how to dance?"

"Um, yeah?" Presley blinked. "Not to bring up a

sore subject, but didn't everyone see that at his wedding? It's pretty impressive."

"No," the entire table said at once.

"He had one slow dance with his ex-wife," Harlan said. "And besides the fact we weren't fans of Elena, the dance was fucking painful to watch."

"And if memory serves me correctly." Lane tapped Waylen on the shoulder. "You made a big deal about not wanting a big wedding or reception. You and Elena fought over that, right?"

"We fought over a lot of shit." Waylen sat up. "She wanted a big freaking spectacle, and I wanted to elope. We compromised, including my agreement that I would twirl her around the dance floor once, but wouldn't ever climb back on it."

Kian leaned closer to Presley. "He really knows how to cut a rug?"

"Mostly country line dancing," Presley said.

"You've got to be fucking with us." Raider stared at her with wide eyes.

"You wanna see?" She stood.

"They do not." Waylen pinched her knee. "Sit down."

The boys pounded the table. "Dance, dance, dance," they shouted.

Presley scurried over to the jukebox.

"Babe, you can play the song, but I'm not getting on that dance floor," Waylen said. "I haven't done that shit in years and I don't plan on making a fool of myself now."

She found the song—their song—and pressed the buttons. She turned, lowered her chin, wiggled her finger, and shook her hips. "Achy Breaky Heart" blasted through the speakers.

The whole thing took her mind off everything. It was exactly what she needed, and Waylen's friends were nothing to be jealous of.

Even if they ripped him off this island, they were kind, honorable men who adored Waylen and would lay down their lives for him and those he cared for, which included her.

She felt that to her core the moment she stood at the edge of that table.

Whether Waylen stayed on this island with her or followed his team around the globe, she'd finally found the closure—no, she couldn't call it that; it was more like life had come full circle with regard to Waylen. Her heart had been healed from the open wound that had never been properly stitched.

They had always loved each other and probably always would.

Even if they were never meant to be together.

10

"*A*re you going to dance with the lady, or are you going to be a dick and leave her hanging?"

Waylen lowered his chin and glared at Blake. He blinked. "Fine," he muttered, pushing to his feet and ignoring his buddies' hoots and hollers. He took Presley's hand. "I'm going to get you back for this one." He turned and kept his focus on her, and not his idiot friends.

He waited for the right moment, before stepping into the line dance.

If this made her happy, made her forget all her problems for two and a half minutes, then it was well worth the razzing he'd get from his teammates.

Anything for Presley.

He'd given her his heart a long time ago and when he left Big Island, he left a large part of himself with Presley. He'd tried to deny it for years, but standing on this dance floor like he had so many years ago, all the love he had for her came crashing down.

The dance wasn't anything special. Or difficult. It was one of those things that everyone did on social media and it had been around for decades. Some did it better than others and oddly, he knew he fell into the better category, but because it was one more thing that the cool kids picked on him about, he kept his dancing feet to himself.

Lane whistled.

Raider and Kian clapped. Loudly.

And Harlan, well, he was on his feet, stomping and yelling, which was entirely out of character for that man, but Waylen appreciated the support.

Most importantly, Presley smiled and laughed. She looked light, and that made his heart sing. He wanted to give her the world. He needed to protect her from anything and anyone who might cause her harm.

His cell vibrated in his back pocket. He ignored it until the song was over, except everyone on his team paused to glance at theirs. It was Kian who waved his in the air with a cocked brow, a tilted head, and a frown.

Waylen yanked his phone out and tapped the screen, pulling up the group text from Mano. "Fuck," he mumbled.

"What is it?" Presley gripped his forearm, peering over his shoulder.

"It's Vernon. He's headed in this direction. Not sure if he's actually got the balls to show his face here, but—"

"Trust me, he's got the kahunas." Presley stormed off toward the table. She waved her hand in the air. "Hey, Lisa, I need a couple of shots of tequila."

"Bad day, huh?" Lisa waved from across the bar.

"Anytime Vernon's involved, it's the fucking worst." Presley yanked her chair back and plopped herself into it, leaning back. "I warned you that I shouldn't be ignoring his texts."

"There's no reason for you to speak to him." Waylen stood behind her, massaging her shoulder with one hand, his cell in the other. "If Vernon decides to come inside, I want to disperse some."

"What do you mean?" Raider asked as Lisa set a round of shots and fresh drinks on the table.

"Vernon doesn't know any of us except Presley and Blake," Waylen said.

Presley shook her head. "He's seen pictures of you." She glanced over her shoulder and winced. "Between that thing hanging over the bar and pictures my parents kept, he knows exactly what you look like and who you were to me and my parents."

"That's fine. I want that fucker to know me," Waylen said. "Harlan and Raider, I want you two

171

sitting at the bar. One at each end. Lane, I want you near the exit in the back. Me, Presley, Kian, and Blake will sit right here, and if Vernon wants to chat, he can do it with us. Mano's going to stay in the parking lot." His phone vibrated. He glanced at the screen. "Vernon just pulled in."

"It's possible he's already got eyes here," Harlan said. "Moving around might not do what you want it to."

"Maybe not, but let's do it anyway. At least we'll have the exits covered, and we'll be prepared for anything." Waylen reached over Presley, setting his phone on the table. "Keep an eye out for any odd movement."

Lane, Raider, and Harlan quickly shuffled to their new spots in the restaurant.

Waylen eased into the chair, draping his arm around Presley. His cell lit up with another text from Mano.

Waylen quickly checked it. "Vernon's banging on your door."

"He knows I come here sometimes after I close up shop," Presley said. "My parents did it when I was a kid and I kept up the tradition. Sadly, Vernon and I did it when we were married, and I wasn't about to stop. This place has been a constant in my life."

"I know, babe," Waylen whispered. It would only be a few minutes before Vernon showed his face. Waylen held her gaze for a long moment, contemplating how to address what he wanted to express. He let out a quick breath.

"Whatever's on your mind, just spit it out." Presley folded her arms.

He craned his neck. "Whatever you do, don't shoot your mouth off. Don't antagonize him." He winced. The Presley he knew back in the day didn't like to be told what to do by her peers, or by anyone for that matter. He imagined she wouldn't take too kindly to him managing her behavior when it came to her ex-husband.

"You might have to hog-tie me and duct-tape my mouth." Presley lifted one of the shots and dropped it back like it was nothing. She picked up a second one, but he grabbed her hand before she could toss it back.

"Go easy on those," Waylen said. "I'm not trying to control you. It's just that you can be——"

She leaned in and kissed his cheek. "I appreciate you looking out for me. And you're right. That's only going to bring out the worst side of me. I'll save the second one for when the jerk leaves."

"That's my girl." He kissed her tenderly.

The door swung open.

She gripped his hand.

Waylen turned, sucking in a deep breath. He'd seen pictures of Vernon, but seeing him in person brought a visceral response that Waylen wasn't prepared for. Every nerve ending in his body exploded. It wasn't a little prickle. An annoyance that needed to be dealt with. It was more like a fucking disaster had waltzed into his life.

Vernon represented destruction.

Waylen felt that deep in his bones.

On the outside Vernon was a striking man. Devilishly handsome. He stood approximately six foot, give or take an inch. He had dark hair, brown eyes, and he carried himself with confidence.

The hair on the back of Waylen's neck stood at attention.

Vernon paused at the entrance and scanned the room. When he did that, there was a lull in the action. It was as if he sucked up the energy in the room so everyone would take notice.

And they did.

He was the kind of man who commanded a room without trying. Based on the way he smiled and waved to Lisa, women would most certainly find him attractive and inevitably charming.

She wasn't impressed, but it would be easy to fall for his twinkling eyes and dazzling smile to those who didn't know his history.

He homed in on Presley and sauntered in their direction. His strides were long. He glanced side to side with each step as if to take in the ambiance.

But Waylen knew that's not what Vernon was

doing. No. This was the walk of an arrogant man who was making sure his presence was being noted.

Dick.

It would take a miracle for Waylen not to beat the shit out of this asshole.

"Relax, babe." He took her hand and lifted it to his lips.

"You're one to talk." She arched a brow. "I can feel the tension flowing through your veins. It's like I'm sitting right next to Kilauea seconds before her most violent eruption."

He swallowed. Hard.

"Presley," Vernon said. "I stopped by the office and your place. When you weren't there, I figured you might be here."

"What do you want?" Presley asked, folding her arms.

Waylen wasn't sure if the way she closed herself off was a good sign or not, but he knew Presley well enough to know she was one hot button from telling Vernon to fuck off.

"I've been worried about you. But you haven't responded to my messages or answered my calls." Vernon shifted his gaze around the table before landing back on Presley. "I'd like to speak to you, in private."

"Not going to happen." Waylen willed his pulse to settle, if that was possible. "She has nothing to say to you."

Vernon looked Waylen up and down. "Never in a million years did I think I'd meet the man my wife named a boat and a cat after, but here we are."

"She's your ex-wife, and we're in the middle of a nice evening. Now, if you don't mind—"

"I do mind," Vernon interrupted Waylen. "I'm shocked that she's letting you speak for her. She hates that, don't you, sweetie."

"I'm not your sweetie, so don't call me that," Presley said, clenching her fists. "After everything that has happened, I can't believe you'd come here and believe we have anything to say to one another or that I'd even want to hear you out. Unless you're ready to make good on selling me my family business, leave me the fuck alone."

"For the record, I heard about the break-in and just wanted to ensure you were okay. I've been concerned for your safety. I've never liked you living out here alone."

Presley jumped to her feet. "You've got some fucking nerve to say that to me after the hell you put me through." She waggled her finger in Vernon's face.

Shit. The last thing Waylen needed was Presley to get all riled up and for Vernon to react.

Swiftly, he rose, looping his arm around her waist, hoisting her close. He pressed his lips against her temple. "Shhhh, let's not go there," he whispered.

She tilted her head and glared.

He wasn't about to back down and let her go head-to-head with Vernon. It served no purpose.

"Well, aren't you two just adorable." Vernon planted his hands on his hips. "Come on, Presley. We have some things to discuss."

"Whatever you want to say to Presley, you can do it with me present." Waylen puffed out his chest.

"This is between me and my wife," Vernon said.

"Ex-wife," Waylen corrected for the second time. "And my presence is nonnegotiable."

Vernon planted his hands on his hips. "Fine. You want to pound your chest and play bodyguard for no reason, I'll go along." He shifted his gaze back to Presley. "I get you're mad at me, but I don't understand why you're lying to the police. It will only hurt you and *our* business in the long run. Is that what you want, Presley? Because I doubt that's what your parents would want."

"You are a fucking asshole." Presley lunged forward. "Don't you dare bring my parents into this."

Waylen grabbed her by the waist and lifted her off the ground, stopping her from taking a swing at her ex.

"You're the liar." She waved her finger. "It's all you've ever done since the day I met you."

"Presley, he's not worth it," Waylen whispered in her ear, setting her feet back on the floor. He gripped her by the shoulders and locked gazes. "Don't give him any ammunition, okay? He wants to get you all riled up and come out swinging in a room full of witnesses."

Presley stared at Waylen with wide eyes. She blinked a few times, but what he said hadn't registered yet.

Blake came up behind Presley and placed a hand on her back. "He's right, you know."

Presley let out a long breath and nodded.

Waylen turned. "You got what you came for; now leave us alone."

"Actually, I haven't." Vernon folded his arms. "I'm part owner in Driftwood Tours. There's a lot of damage control that needs to be done because of what happened. I've recently learned that there have been cancellations, and we need to come up with a—"

"You've got to be fucking kidding me," Presley mumbled. "I've always run the day-to-day. You sit back and take my money. That's about it and it's not going to change now. There's nothing for you to do."

"That's not true and you know it," Vernon said. "And thanks to your lies about me, I'm dealing with other issues. We need to figure this out so our business can survive. I'm not leaving until we have a conversation about how to do that and I'm not having it with this asshole." He pointed to

Waylen. "He's not family and he has no skin in this game."

Kian was on his feet in a flash.

Waylen raised his hand, indicating Kian needed to stand down.

"I'm not fucking going anywhere. I'm more like family than you have ever been and you don't ever want to find out what me and my buddy over there do when we have even a tiny bit of skin in the game." Waylen widened his stance. "If you don't like where the investigation is heading, take it up with the cops. Not us. Until then, she still owns more of that business than you do, and according to your divorce settlement, which I've seen, it's her call. We're going to sit back down and enjoy our night. I can't tell you to leave this establishment, but if you keep bothering us, or her, I will remove you."

"Are you threatening me?" Vernon dared to smile. "Because that sounded like a threat and I would advise against doing that."

Waylen matched it with a grin. "I'm simply stating facts."

"You think because you're some hotshot SEAL or some such shit that you can push me around? Well, I'm not afraid of you," Vernon said. "Or your pansy-ass friend over there."

Waylen leaned closer, his blood boiling in his veins. He wanted to punch this fucker right between the eyes. But that would make him no better than

Vernon and Waylen wasn't going to stoop to his level. "I'm not asking you to be afraid, although we're not the kind of men you want to fuck with. However, I'm asking you nicely to leave us alone. I'm not going to ask twice. If you choose to keep pushing our buttons, I'll call the cops. I don't think you want us to go that route. Not while all this is under investigation." He arched a brow. "Presley doesn't want you around, right, babe?"

"Damn fucking straight I don't," she said.

"There you go." Waylen pointed to the door. "If something comes up about the business that she needs to notify you about or discuss with you, she'll call you. But outside of that, stay away from my girl-friend. Have I made myself clear?"

"Your *threat* is crystal clear." Vernon smiled. "Presley, I'll send you an email about everything that needs to be taken care of if we're going to weather this storm."

"You mean the insane problems you created for us," Presley said under her breath. "Don't fucking bother."

"Have a nice night." Hoping that would be the end of it, Waylen planted his ass in a chair with his hand resting on Presley's thigh. He squeezed. Tightly.

Vernon didn't budge. "Call off your watchdog, Mano. I know he's been following me. I don't like it and it's harassment. If it continues, I'll have him arrested. And don't think for one second I won't. If he follows me out of this parking lot, the first thing I will do is call our good buddy Hale." Vernon spun on his heel and sauntered toward the door.

"I'm sorry. I can't control my tongue around that douchebag." Presley reached for the second shot and downed it.

"I don't blame you for that. He's a prick." Waylen curled his fingers around her wrist. He blinked. "Please make that your last shot."

"You're probably right, but my nerves are completely unsettled. I don't understand what point he was trying to get across or what he wanted. It served nothing," Presley said. "And can he do that to Mano?"

"It's borderline stalking," Kian said. "But he'd have to prove all sorts of malice and intent. It's a whole gray area."

"He said that to scare us, but I'm not afraid. Vernon had an agenda, and it all started with who you were hanging around with." Waylen picked up his cell and quickly read the text from Mano. "This was all about checking me and my men out. Getting a read on us. A facial recognition. And perhaps to see if Mano or anyone else was actually following him." Waylen craned his neck.

"What do you want to do?" Kian asked.

"Outsmart the asshole." Waylen waved to

Raider. "I'm going to step outside as if to check to make sure Vernon left."

"You mean he hasn't?" Presley stared at him with daggers shooting from her beautiful blue eyes.

"He's leaning against the hood of his vehicle, tapping away on his cell," Waylen said. "I'm guessing he wants me to come outside. Either he wants to get his ass kicked or this is a power play."

"I've seen his kind before," Kian said. "My money's on the latter."

"Mine too," Waylen nodded. "Based on that assumption, he could be hoping I'll call off Mano in front of him or see if I'm willing to flex my muscles. But all he'll get to do is watch Mano drive off."

"So, you're going to let Vernon go without anyone watching him?" Presley stared at him like a doe in headlights.

"No fucking way." He dug into his pocket and handed Raider his keys. "You know what to do."

"On it."

"Harlan, you take backup." Waylen made the whirlybird motion.

"Going out the back door." Harlan nodded.

He leaned over and brushed his lips over Presley's mouth. "Mano's going to take overwatch of your place tonight. My friends are going to tail Vernon. Don't you worry. That dickface comes anywhere near this marina, he's in for a world of hurt."

She grabbed his shirt. "Thank you."

"I got your back." Twenty-three years ago, he boarded a plane for Maryland with his mom. He'd been heartbroken over his father's death and the girl he'd left behind. He'd been seventeen and he hadn't a choice.

He loved her back then and he loved her even more today.

This time he wasn't leaving.

Presley leaned over the railing and stared out at the star-filled sky. A breeze rolled in off the ocean. When Waylen had left Big Island twenty-three years ago, her dreams of being with him had still been alive in her soul, but her heart and mind were conflicted.

Encouraging him to stay on his path to the Naval Academy and becoming a SEAL was the right thing to do.

For him.

When she heard he had graduated, part of her waited for the letter or call stating he wanted her to come join him wherever he was in the world.

But it never came.

"You shouldn't be out here alone," Blake's voice bellowed in the night air.

"Waylen knows where I am." She jerked her

thumb over her shoulder. "He hasn't let me out of his sight since Vernon left."

"He's full of surprises, that one." Blake rested her hip against the rail. "He and everyone on his team are good men."

"I won't argue with that statement." A gust of wind came in off the water, rattling the sheets against the masts of the sailboats in the marina. It was sweet music to her ears. As a little girl, she loved to come down to the docks and sit and listen to it for hours. "You and Kian seem chummy."

"I wouldn't go that far, but he was incredibly helpful during the rescue."

Presley hadn't known Blake for very long, but in their time together, Blake had become one of Presley's closest friends. It wasn't a typical girl friendship. Then again, Presley didn't have many of those throughout her life. Most of her friends growing up had been men. She struggled to relate to women. Her father used to tell her it was because she threatened most of the other girls her age and when she got older, it would change.

Sadly, it never did.

"Kian and Waylen seem tight," Blake said. "Like they have a bromance going on. But then I saw Waylen with Lane and thought the same thing."

Presley laughed. "Waylen's like that with all the guys on the team. I just met them, but the way he talks about them, they're his family. He doesn't do anything without them. They retired together, and whatever is next for them in civilian life, they will do it as a team."

"How do you feel about that?" Blake asked.

Presley shrugged. "Same way as I did when Waylen had to leave Big Island. It's not about me."

"That's different. You were kids. Are you really going to let him walk out of your life this time without telling him what you want?" Blake asked. "Because it's obvious how much you care about him and want him to stay."

"I can't ask him to stay. That's ridiculous. We're completely different people. Just because we've had a little fun reconnecting and reminiscing about how things used to be, doesn't mean there's anything substantial there. He and his friends have a plan, and I won't be the person who blows it up."

"And who are you trying to sell that line of bull-shit to? Me or yourself?" Blake poked her arm. "Besides, I see how he looks at you. The man has it bad."

"All you see is history."

"No. I see two people who have feelings for each other that never died. At the very least, it warrants a few conversations." Blake cocked her head. "Unless there's something else you're not telling me."

There were a few details she'd left out and she wasn't about to share them with anyone. "Until this shit with Vernon is wrapped up, I'm not about to put pressure on Waylen about anything. Between dealing with all this and an IT job he's working on for the Brotherhood Protectors, he's got enough on his plate without me adding to it."

"Why do you always do that?"

Presley stood tall and stared at her friend. "Do what?"

"Put everyone else before yourself," Blake said. "I've watched you do it with Remi and his wife. All your employees. With Lisa and Al. Even with Mano, who doesn't need shit. You take care of everyone, making sure their needs are met. When are you going to take care of yourself?"

"You don't think divorcing Vernon was putting myself first?" Presley asked with a raised voice. She hadn't meant to sound angry, but leaving that asshole had been one of the hardest things she'd ever done.

"I didn't say that." Blake raised her hands. "I wasn't around when that happened. I only know what you told me, and don't get pissed. But you didn't do it until you were left with no choice. And I'm not judging. You were busy taking care of your parents. I get it. I really do. You have the biggest heart of anyone I know. You're the one person most people can say that if they were to call at three in the morning, you'd pick up the damn phone. Hell, a stranger could call you, and you'd be out the door in a flash. But who are you calling?"

Presley opened her mouth but shut it right quick. Blake was right. She could name a few people that would.

Mano.

Remi.

Blake.

Even Waylen.

It wasn't as if she didn't have friends. She had damn fucking good ones. But they were few and far between.

The reality was that she never called anyone until it was too late. Mano had already given her that lecture.

She'd like to blame her father, who raised her to be independent and self-reliant. He wanted his little girl to be able to fend for herself. He taught her all about cars. She knew how to change her own oil and deal with a flat tire. By the time she was twelve, she could man a vessel by herself.

It had been both a blessing and a curse.

Like Waylen being teased for being smart, she had been picked on relentlessly for being a tomboy.

Blake placed her hand on Presley's shoulder. "I know it's hard for you to rely on the help of others."

"I'm taking the help," Presley said. "I never thought I'd say this, but I'm actually fucking terrified of Vernon and what he might be capable of. He put my damn cat in a dumpster. Who does that but a person who doesn't care about a living, breathing creature."

"Little Waylen is in good hands at Mano's place."

"We're calling him Way-Way now." Presley chuckled. "Every time I call the cat, Waylen thinks I'm calling him to bed, and it gets weird."

"I imagine it would." Blake nodded. "I'm sorry all this is happening, but I'm glad you're not resisting Waylen and his friends."

"Even if I was, Waylen is more stubborn than I am. However, I know his controlling and commanding ways come from a good place. He's not trying to keep me down."

"He cares about you, and you'd have to be blind not to see it." Blake squeezed her shoulder. "I told the guys I'm available if they need anything from me."

"I appreciate that."

"I'm a text or phone call away. Remember that."

Presley wasn't the kind of person who hugged her friends, but she found herself in a warm embrace with Blake. "Thank you for being there for me and rescuing my sorry ass."

"Here comes Waylen," Blake whispered. "I'll talk with you tomorrow." She strolled off the dock and headed toward Kian, passing Waylen on the way, pausing for a moment.

Presley couldn't hear their brief conversation. She trusted Blake to keep her confidence. Not that they had discussed anything earth-shattering, but still, Presley wasn't ready to pour her heart and soul into Waylen.

Loving him had always been easy, and that hadn't changed.

Telling him she wanted him to stay on Big Island and give them a second chance was something entirely different.

11

"*How* are you feeling, babe?" Waylen leaned in and kissed Presley's cheek. He adjusted his backpack, which housed his computer and a bottle of wine. The past and the present collided in his mind as he stood under the starry sky. Tall sailing masts danced under the moon. He'd kissed her for the first time on the docks at this very marina.

He remembered it like it was yesterday.

He'd been all of thirteen years old and it had been one of the best days of his young life.

"That's an odd question."

He placed his free hand on her back and nudged her toward the dock. "You had a lot to drink. Just doing a little check on that."

"My buzz is gone. I had a lot of water after

190

Vernon left." She stepped onto the dock. "Where are we going?"

"Mano's boat."

"That thing ain't a boat. It's a yacht."

Waylen dug his hand into his pocket. "Well, I got the key and permission to board." He smiled wide. "That man has more toys than any human should be allowed."

"I'm so glad he finally found a nice girl who isn't after his money."

"Bella seems cool," Waylen said. "I get the feeling Mano's been a bit lost since his parents died."

"That's putting it mildly. He was devastated when their plane went down, and he holds himself responsible."

"Why?"

"He was supposed to go with them, and he has this stupid notion that the outcome might have been different if he'd been with them. Or he would have died with them. Survivor's guilt had a huge grip on him until he met Bella. She pulled him from a serious depression. However, he struggles with all that money. He doesn't know what to do with it, or with himself sometimes."

"Al told me he's started a few foundations and charities and tried to help you pay off Vernon."

"That's money I would have taken, only Vernon

wouldn't let me buy him out. At least not when I divorced him."

"That's what doesn't make sense to me." Waylen stopped in front of the big yacht at the end of the dock. "Jesus. This is a floating house."

"Wait until you see inside. It's got all the bells and whistles. Mano could barely maneuver it through the channel when he first bought it. I had to show him how to do it."

"I bet you had fun showing off your skills." Waylen opened the side gate and held Presley's hand while she boarded. He took the key and unlocked the galley. "Let's sit on the deck and enjoy a glass of wine."

"Aren't we on high alert?"

"Harlan and Raider have eyes on Vernon. Mano's sitting outside your place. The rest of my team is overlooking all the weak spots at the marina. I've got some work to do on my computer to get ahead of whatever Vernon has planned, but Vernon isn't doing anything tonight."

"How can you be so sure?" She climbed up the ladder toward the bow.

"I'm not." He followed, easing onto one of the lounge beds and taking out the bottle and two plastic glasses. "But I trust that my team has it covered, so let's relax for a little bit. Besides, I do want to talk to you about a few things." He poured the wine and handed her a glass. "I spoke to Hale after the incident at Al and Lisa's."

"And?" She brought the glass to her lips and sipped. The way the light from the moon caught her hair took his breath away.

"Frank's still in a medically induced coma and the doctors can't give him a date on when they will try to pull him out so he can interview him." All Waylen wanted to do was take her into his arms and love her the way she deserved. She was the kindest and most caring human he'd ever met outside of his mother and his team. But he had to set aside his emotions for the moment. "Everyone on that charter is sticking with their story, saying that they know nothing about a deal between Frank and Vernon."

Presley opened her mouth, but he hushed her by pressing his finger over her plump, sweet lips. "Hale did learn that Frank has a *lending* business."

"What does that mean?"

"Exactly how it sounds. He lends money to people and expects to get his money back on a certain date. When he doesn't get it, he puts a certain kind of pressure on his clients and it's not the kind a bank would."

"That makes Frank sound like a bad man," Presley said.

Waylen set his glass on the fancy drink holder

and pulled out his computer. "That's where my skills come in handy. I can peek inside places Hale wouldn't dare go legally."

"I don't want you to get in trouble."

Waylen chuckled. "I won't. You have to remember this is what I did for a living for the government when I wasn't deployed on missions. I might not have the security clearance I used to have, but I have friends in high places." He winked. "All I need is to give Hale a connection between Frank and Vernon so Hale can take his investigation to the next level."

"You think Vernon was trying to get out of paying Frank back money? That's why he tried to blow up my boat? With me and innocent people on it?"

"Unfortunately, that's only step one." He lifted her chin with his thumb. "Vernon's not stupid, but he's not as smart as I am. When you make a new will, it has to be signed by you, two witnesses, and generally, it has to be notarized if you don't want it challenged. Vernon was smart enough to do that."

"Wait. What?" She bolted upright, sloshing her wine all down the front of her shirt. "Shit." She wiped her chest. "He actually made a new will? For me? How do you know that?"

"It took some digging on my part." He flipped open his computer and pulled up the new document. "The two witnesses are Herb Buckley and Jessica Leroy. Do you know either of them?"

"Yeah. Herb is one of his old business partners when he worked selling time-shares and Jessica is the chick he cheated on me with."

"That's fucking cold," Waylen muttered. "I need to send this document to Hale along with your actual will, but not until I've had a friend finish their analysis of your signature. If there's even a remote possibility that Vernon got you to sign something—"

"Don't even finish that statement because I will hurt you if you do." She glared. "I look over everything that man sends me. I don't sign one fucking thing without reading the fine print."

"Babe, I wasn't going to say you did. But that doesn't mean he couldn't have slipped your signature onto something. As I said, he's not stupid, and there are ways to forge a person's signature properly. I won't put you or your parents' family business at stake without having all our ducks in a row."

She leaned back and closed her eyes. "How could I have ever been married to such a snake. I look at him, and all I have is hatred in my heart. What did I ever see in him?"

Waylen set his computer to the side. He wrapped his arm around Presley and pulled her tight. "I often wonder the same thing about Elena."

"She didn't cut the gas line on your boat and nearly kill you."

"Nope. But she made my life a living hell for a few years." There were so many things about his marriage that he never told anyone except Kian and Lane. He certainly didn't tell his mother.

She would have gone into Mama Bear mode and ripped Elena a new one.

Elena wasn't worth it.

"I'm sorry, but I don't see how fighting over a piano is the same."

He chuckled. "Honestly, that was the least of our problems. And it wasn't just about my unwillingness to retire early. Or even my bond with my team. When Elena and I first met, she made me believe she was on board with my career. She quit her job and relocated from Virginia to Florida before we even got married. And then again to California shortly after."

"That's what a Navy wife does. I'm sure it wasn't easy, especially when you were a SEAL and being deployed."

"It's not, but that first move seemed to go flawlessly. I thought she was happy. Outside of our very different ideas about a wedding, we got along great. The second move didn't go so well. She dug her heels in and demanded I not re-enlist when my contract came up. She told me she'd leave me if I did."

"But she didn't."

He burst out laughing. "Actually, she did. I

brought the papers home and told her I wasn't ready and that it was unfair of her to ask me to do that after I'd worked so hard to get where I was. She packed a bag and flew back to Virginia. I left for parts unknown and was gone for six weeks. When I came home, I expected it would be to an empty house. Only, she was there. Begging for my forgiveness, but that came with a price."

"How can one place a price on forgiveness?"

"She would stay, and we'd work out our martial issues, if I promised that at the end of that contract, that would be it and I would give her a baby."

"What did you say?"

"I don't like to fail at anything," he said. "So I agreed, except the idea of becoming a father made me cringe under those circumstances, and let's just say I avoided sex. Of course, I was gone a lot, which didn't help."

"No offense, but this still isn't the same."

"I'm getting to the similarities." He lifted his glass and sipped. "When I finally realized we were both miserable, I came home and told her that I wanted a divorce. She was so pissed she took a hammer and smashed all the windows on my brand-new pickup. She pawned her wedding ring and mother's engagement ring."

"That bitch. Your mom must have lost her mind."

"I found the pawn shop and paid a ridiculous amount of money to get it back."

"I'm sorry you had to do that. Elena should have given it back. It's a family thing," Presley said.

His heart beat so fast it got stuck in his throat. *Ring. Family.* All the confusion of why his mother wanted him to bring the damn thing with him filled his soul. He shoved the conflicting thoughts from his mind. This had nothing to do with his mom and her strange request.

"Elena wanted to hurt me and part of me understands why. She gave up her life in Virginia to be married to me, and it wasn't what she had expected, although I'm not exactly sure how she couldn't have known. Her father was Air Force. She knew the drill."

"Did she do anything else?"

"Yup," he admitted. "While I was deployed during our separation, she gave away my dog. She gave all my clothes to Goodwill, and she listed that damn fucking piano on the internet for sale. One of our mutual friends emailed me that juicy piece of information."

"She's vindictive."

Waylen nodded. "Now that she's remarried, I don't have to deal with her. But the divorce was ugly as hell. I don't wish it on anyone. I swore after that I'd never get tangled up with another woman again." He kissed her temple. "But here I am, holding you, and all I can think about is all the what-ifs of the past and the possibilities of the future."

Presley rested her head on his chest. "Seeing you again, seeing the kind of man you've become, I have to believe I did the right thing by you." She glanced up. Tears welled in her eyes. "I didn't write that last letter to hurt you. It wasn't that I didn't love and care about you. We were a million miles apart. You had to follow that dream. Being a SEAL is all you've ever wanted."

He shifted, taking her face with his hands. "Babe, my only regret regarding all that is not reaching out after graduation. Or any time after that. I'd thought about it so many times. You were right about me needing to do that. But I should have followed more than my career aspirations. I should have followed my heart, because I left it here with you." He stared into her eyes, hoping to find the same deep passion.

She palmed his cheek. "You're a very sweet man."

"I'm being serious."

"I know and that's what scares me."

"Why?" He traced his finger across her lower lip. At seventeen, or even twenty-one, he had so much life ahead of him that moving on without her seemed somewhat possible. But at forty? He knew he couldn't do it again and be content, much less happy.

"I can't ask you to turn your back on your friends or the dreams you've created with them to stay here on Big Island with me. It's not fair to you or them."

"You're not asking me to do anything." He lifted her chin. "Three of my buddies have found ladies they don't want to leave behind. And have you seen the way Kian and Blake look at each other? There's most definitely something brewing there. And even if none of them had a connection to the opposite sex, we've all been talking about wanting to stay."

"But there's something else that's pulling you to stay and that's your sense of duty and responsibility. I won't have it."

"Oh, for fuck's sake, Presley. Sure, the fact we've been irresponsible when it comes to using birth control is in the back of my mind. But it has no bearing on wanting to be with you. To have a second chance with you."

"Bullshit." She pressed her hands on his chest and inched away. "You forget how well I know you and how honorable you are."

He couldn't believe he was going to do this. Not even Kian or Lane knew. A fair amount of shame still filled his soul regarding how he'd handled leaving Elena and the circumstances surrounding it. But what the hell? "You don't know me as well as you think you do, and I can prove how wrong you really are."

"Yeah. How?"

"The day I told Elena I wanted a divorce, she told me she was pregnant." Waylen reached for the wine bottle and topped off his glass. He downed half of it. Saying the words out loud made his chest burn. That day hadn't been one of his shining moments. As a matter of fact, it made him the biggest asshole on the planet.

"Excuse me?"

"You heard me."

"What came first? The *I want a divorce* or the *we're going to have a baby*?"

"She told me she was pregnant, and instead of being a supportive husband, I told her I didn't love her anymore and it was over. That I would be a good father, if the kid was mine, but she and I were done."

"Jesus, you're an asshole. Although, I do want to revisit the question of paternity."

"Trust me, I know what a dick I was. I've apologized to her for my timing, but it will never make up for it."

"So, you are a father?" Presley blinked. Her lips parted. Her face contorted as if she swallowed a lemon.

He shook his head. "No. Turns out it was an ectopic pregnancy. She'll tell you that it was all my fault and I don't blame her for that. My mother explained to me what ectopic meant, because I had no idea, so in reality, I didn't have anything to do with what happened, but I still feel guilty as hell." He raised his finger. "And to answer that burning question, I'll never know if it was mine or not."

"She stepped out on your marriage?"

"Elena had an affair near the end of the marriage. I was gone so much, and all we did was fight, but she swore the baby was mine. I did the math on when she got pregnant, and it didn't really add up. Still, that doesn't erase the way I went about things."

Presley straddled his legs, took his glass from his hand, and set it aside. "It certainly does not. But do you think that maybe when she informed you of its existence, you reacted the way you did because, deep down, you knew the baby wasn't yours?"

"That's what my mom thinks."

"I've always thought your mother was one smart cookie."

He laughed. "I'm shocked you don't hate me after that revelation."

"I'm not sure I could hate you if I tried." She leaned in and kissed him softly. "I need you to promise me that any consideration you have about staying on Big Island will have nothing to do with whether or not I'm pregnant."

"I can't make that promise," he whispered.

"Because if you are, of course it will. But what I can promise is that I've already decided that staying is what I want. If the Brotherhood Protectors offers us a job, we're taking it. If not, I'm going to find another way. This is my home." He batted her nose. "And I've already asked my mom to move back too."

Presley jerked her head.

"See, I told you I was serious and that—"

"Shut up and kiss me."

He took her mouth in a hot, wet kiss. Their tongues wrapped around each other's in a wild, familiar dance. He squeezed her ass, molding his fingers into her flesh. "We better take this down below."

"I like sex under the stars."

"So do I. But I have team members with binoculars on rooftops."

She jumped to her feet and scurried around the side of the boat and down the ladder. "What are you waiting for?"

Snagging his computer, he stuffed it in his backpack. He'd deal with the wine and glasses later.

It took all of four minutes to make it into the master state suite. He pushed open the door and his jaw dropped as he stared at Presley sprawled out on the bed.

Naked.

"I like grown-up, Presley."

She laughed. "As if I had all that much shame and modesty when I was a teenager."

"That's a true statement." He set his bag on the dresser, kicked off his shoes, and shed his clothing. Pulling back the sheets, he climbed into bed with the only woman he'd ever loved.

And the only woman he would ever need.

Wrapping his arm around her, he pulled her close, their bodies melding together like two halves of a single soul. The moonlight shined through the porthole and cast a soft glow on her face, illuminating the delicate curves and features that he had come to know and love so intimately. She was his beacon, his anchor, his everything.

Her tender caresses and breathless whispers filled the room with an intoxicating energy. The dangers that lurked outside faded away as their passion and affection for one another created a cocoon of intimacy that defied time and space.

With each tender touch and gentle kiss, the intensity of their love grew, fueling the flames of desire that had burned unabated for years.

He brushed a lock of hair from her cheek, tracing its soft curves with his fingertips. He'd never tire of loving her, ever.

Their bodies moved in perfect sync, as if their souls were speaking a language only they could comprehend. The room seemed to pulsate with the rhythm of their passion, and Presley's intense moans whispered against his skin in the sweetest of aftershocks.

As their passion reached its peak, he whispered her name over and over again. He wanted her to feel loved. Adored. Appreciated. Valued.

Their bodies moved together like dancers, locked in an eternal waltz, as they found release in each other's embrace.

The world outside no longer mattered. He was home, with the one woman who could make him feel complete.

She rested her head on his chest, draping her arm and leg over his body.

Running his fingers through her soft hair, he stared out the porthole. The idea of becoming a dad when he'd been married had been utterly terrifying. It wasn't that he didn't believe he'd be a good father. It had more to do with the fact his marriage had already failed. As a couple, they weren't equipped to be parents.

But him and Presley?

That was a question he honestly wasn't sure he had the answer to. They fit together. He loved her, even if he hadn't said the words out loud, and he believed that love was reciprocated.

However, it took more than love to make a family.

"We're following a pattern." He turned, pressing his lips against her temple. "Freud would have a field day with us, especially after all we've discussed."

"To be totally honest with you, I'm not all that stressed over it."

"Really? Why's that?"

"It took a year for me to get pregnant. After that, Vernon and I tried for another three years and didn't use birth control for the rest of our marriage. I never got pregnant again. I'm almost forty and as regular as I am with my periods, I feel like it's something that's not meant to be for me."

"But having a child is something you want." His heart hammered in his chest. He'd given up the idea of marriage, kids, family a long time ago and he'd been okay with that.

Not anymore.

He wanted it and he wanted it with Presley.

All of it. The house with a swing set in the backyard. The cute little cat and maybe a dog. Thinking about it made him want to kiss his mother for making him bring that ring.

Damn.

That was a big fucking thought.

But it made him deliriously happy.

"I'm not having this conversation with you."

Gently, he tugged at her hair until their eyes locked. "But it's the truth."

"All right. And what about you? You gave up on

all that. How do you feel about it now?" She arched a brow.

He smiled. "As crazy as it sounds, I still want everything with you."

"It's motherfucking nuts." A tear rolled down her cheek.

"Why are you crying?"

"I can't think about it. Or hope for it. Or anything. My heart was crushed when I lost my baby. It might have been a blessing in disguise, but it doesn't change how it made me feel." She swiped at her face. "I should have stopped you and asked you to wear a condom. I get that. But until I either get my period or pee on a stick and it confirms one way or the other, I can't let my brain go there. Can you understand that at all?"

"Oh, babe. I'm sorry, and I can totally respect that. I won't bring it up again." He made a key sign across his lips and tossed it over his shoulder.

"Well, we will have to discuss—"

He hushed her with a kiss. "Whenever you're ready. Not a second before. Now close your eyes and get some sleep. I have to get up early, but I promise to be quiet."

"Please don't leave me alone."

"If I must step off this yacht, I'll wake you." He kissed her nose.

"Waylen?"

"Yes."

"Since we're saying crazy things, you should know I've never stopped loving you."

"That's the least crazy thing I've heard all day." He held her gaze intently. "I love you, Presley. I always have and I always will."

12

*P*resley stared at the calendar. It had been twelve days since the accident—twelve days since Waylen had come back into her life.

She tapped her pencil against the counter. Her heart beat against her chest. She never had to track her cycle. There hadn't been a need. Before Waylen, she hadn't had sex in over six months and that relationship had lasted all of three weeks.

But she'd been careful.

With Waylen, it was as if they didn't care one way or the other.

She flipped the calendar over, trying desperately to remember the exact date of when she had her last period.

The three-day charter. That was it. Quickly, she

counted the days. Fuck. If that were the case, she should have gotten her period today.

No signs of it at all.

That didn't mean anything. She was under enormous stress. That could affect her cycle. It had in the past. Or at least she wanted to believe it had, although all through her divorce, it hadn't. Nor had her parents' deaths changed her cycle.

But this was different.

Her fucking ex-husband had tried to kill her.

"Hey, babe." Waylen strolled into the office.

She jerked. She hadn't even heard the bell over the door ding. "Shit. You scared me."

"I'm sorry." He leaned over the counter and kissed her tenderly. "What are you doing that has you so engrossed?"

"Nothing really. Just matching up charters in the calendar to receipts." She folded the calendar and tucked it into the drawer. "Any news on Vernon? Frank? The case?"

"Yup." Waylen raked his fingers through his hair. "I got confirmation that your signature on the new will has been considered fraud. I sent all that information over to Hale. He's not happy with me or my methods. But since it came directly from the FBI fraud department, he's got no choice. He has to investigate. This is good news because it gives Vernon a motive. He kills you, he gets the other half of Driftwood Tours. Hale's heading over to

Vernon's right now to have a little chat with him." Waylen let out a short breath. "The bad news is proving that Vernon's the one who did it could be hard."

"How is that even possible?"

"Before I sent it to Hale, my FBI buddy and I did a little investigating on our own. Vernon's lawyer didn't draw up that will. My buddy inquired, and it appears that a woman fitting your description went to a different lawyer's office and filed the paperwork."

"What you're saying is Vernon had someone else do his dirty work."

Waylen nodded. "The good news is that will is null and void."

"Doesn't do any good if I'm dead."

He reached across the counter and took her hand. "Babe, I'm not going to let anything happen to you."

"As long as Vernon is wandering the streets, I'm in danger. You and your friends can't be on watch forever."

"None of us are going anywhere until this is settled. Cassie is over at the hospital waiting for Frank to wake up. Whether or not he's a criminal makes no difference. I doubt he will take too kindly to Vernon trying to kill him either."

"I can't keep asking all of you to—"

"Stop that." He pressed his finger over her lips.

"Besides my buddies doing this for me, it's also a Brotherhood Protectors case now."

"I can't afford them, and I didn't hire them." She cocked her head.

"I did." He lowered his head. "I'm not going to argue with you about this." He yanked his cell out of his back pocket. "It's my mom. She's been dying to talk with you. I've got some things I need to do on my computer. Why don't you chat with her? I'm going to go upstairs for a bit." He tapped his cell and answered the call before she could even open her mouth and protest. "Hey, Ma. How are you doing?" He smiled.

Fuck. FaceTime. That was the last thing she needed.

"Hi, Waylen. I'm good. How are you? How's Presley? She holding up okay? Last we talked, you mentioned some stuff with her—"

"Hey, Mom. I've got a ton of stuff I need to do right now. But Presley's right here." He turned the cell.

Presley smiled and waved.

"Why don't you two ladies catch up. I'll call you later. Love you, Ma."

"Love you too, Waylen," his mom said.

Waylen winked and handed her the phone.

Inwardly, she groaned. "Hi, Sally. It's been a long time." She set the cell against the register and leaned back. "It's good to see you."

"You're as beautiful as I remember." Sally swiped at her cheeks. "I was so sad to hear about your parents. They were such wonderful people. Kind and generous. Always so good to my son."

"Thank you," Presley said. "I miss them very much."

"I'm sure you do." Sally nodded. "Waylen hasn't told me too much about what's going on. Only that your ex-husband has been giving you a hard time. Something about trying to take your parents' business from you."

That was an interesting way of putting it. But she understood Waylen didn't want to worry his poor mom. "It's a long story and I don't want to bore you with the awful details. But Waylen and his team have been incredible."

"They are all good men. They helped Waylen through some bad times. He'd be a lost man without them." Sally waved her finger. "But he's always been a little lost since we left Big Island. I'm so glad he could reconnect with his dad's memories and see you again. I can tell how happy that's made him."

"It's been real good to spend time together." She smiled. Instinctively, she placed a hand over her stomach. "I just hate that some of it is dealing with my ex."

"He wouldn't be there helping if he didn't want to." Sally leaned closer. "That boy of mine never stopped caring about you. I'm so sorry that I didn't have the strength to stay and that I took him away from you."

"Sally, you did what you needed to do for you and your family. Besides, he would have left a year later anyway. It wouldn't have changed the outcome. We all know that. Waylen was meant to have a career as a Navy SEAL and I'm glad he had the opportunity to pursue it."

"Same old Presley. Always putting others before herself," Sally said. "But I can tell you there's been something missing from my son's life. I haven't seen him this happy in a long time and I know it's because he's there with you."

Presley wanted to believe that. Needed to believe that. Last night they had declared their love still lingered. It was real. It had never died. For either of them.

But Presley was a realist. She'd been that way her entire life and she knew love wasn't enough. Strong, lasting relationships were built on so much more and right now, there was too much uncertainty swirling around in her life—and Waylen's—to be confident that they could go the distance.

Stop holding back. Stop being so reserved. If you don't let anyone in, if you don't risk anything again, you'll never find happiness.

Those were her father's words when she'd returned to Big Island after college and made the decision to finally let Waylen go for good.

Of course, he'd wanted her to reach out to Waylen. But he'd also wanted her to start living again. To really expand outside the little world she'd created to protect herself from being hurt.

When she finally allowed herself a chance at love, she let the wrong person in.

She'd vowed never to make that mistake again.

Waylen could never be seen as a mistake. She wouldn't regret this time with him, no matter the outcome.

"Presley, why the long face?" Sally asked.

Presley sighed. "There's a lot going on. Between the problems with the business and…" She couldn't discuss this with Waylen's mom. That was insane. It didn't matter that she'd been a sounding board back when they'd been dating and would fight over stupid stuff.

Like how much he used to fish and be late for a date because he lost track of time.

"What has my son done?" Sally asked.

Presley laughed. "Nothing bad. He's been a perfect gentleman, as always."

"Then what's the problem? Because I know he's working on how to move there. He's even started sending me places to look at online for me to live."

Presley blinked.

"He didn't tell you that?" Sally asked.

"I didn't know he was actively looking." Presley rubbed her belly. When Waylen made up his mind about something, he did it and there was no arguing with him about it either. "He doesn't even know if he has a job here or not. Everything is temporary and up in the air."

"According to him, he and the boys have had some discussions with Hawk, the man who runs the Brotherhood Protectors there and they want to set up a meeting with Hank Patterson, the head of the whole organization. He made it sound like no matter what, he was staying on Big Island, with you. Don't you want that?"

"More than anything," she whispered.

"Have you told him that?"

"I haven't not said it."

"Presley Tina Miles, you have always been an outspoken young lady except for when it comes to two things. What you want and matters of the heart. Do you love my son?"

"Yes, and he knows that." Presley sat up taller.

"Well, that's a start." Sally smiled. "Now tell him you want him to stay. Don't drag your feet. Just do it. Do you hear me?"

"Yes, ma'am."

"All right. I better get going. We'll chat again soon, and before you know it, I'll be back on that island, and we'll do lunch."

"I'd like that. Take care, Sally." She tapped the end button and leaned back.

"That sounded like a nice conversation." Waylen leaned against the doorjamb.

She jumped, nearly falling off the stool. "You have to stop sneaking up on me like that." She tucked her hair behind her ears. "How long have you been standing there?"

"Long enough." He smiled wickedly. "Do you have something to say to me?"

"No," she mumbled. "You're a jerk, you know that. You shouldn't listen in on other people's conversations."

He pointed to the counter. "I needed my phone."

She snagged it and stretched out her arm. "Here. Take it."

He inched closer, wrapping his arm around her waist and heaving her to his chest. "Why is it so hard for you to tell me you want to be with me? That you want me to move here and be in a relationship with me."

"Isn't telling you that I still love you the same thing?"

"Nope. Not even close."

"Fine. I wouldn't mind it if you took a job with the Brotherhood Protectors and you and your crazy band of brothers stayed on Big Island. Does that work for you?" She rested her hands on his shoulders.

"It's a start." He kissed her nose. "Come on. We've got to go."

"Where?"

"To that lawyer who drew up the fake will. Hale's meeting us there."

"Why?" she asked.

"To see if the lawyer recognizes you or not." He took her hand.

"Ugh. I hate this." She reached behind the counter and grabbed her bag.

"It's one step in putting your ex-husband behind bars."

If they accomplished that it would be a fucking miracle.

Waylen leaned against the hood of the car next to Presley. "That went about as expected." He folded his arms. "We need to find this girl who impersonated Presley and tie her back to Vernon."

"That might be like finding a needle in a haystack," Hale said. "Especially when the lawyer denies having any contact with Vernon and both witnesses swear it was Presley who asked them to sign the new will."

"That's bullshit. I did no such thing." Presley leaned into his arm.

"That lawyer stated you weren't the woman who

came to his office and signed the document," Waylen said. "That's something."

"But it doesn't tie Vernon to the crime." Hale arched a brow. "I've got nothing on him at this point."

"I feel like there's something you're not telling us." Waylen wrapped his arm around Presley, resting his hand on her hip. He understood her frustration with the situation. Patience had never been her strong suit.

Hale rubbed his jaw. "There is something my department has been investigating for a bit now that we believe Vernon is involved in. I can't get into the details with you." Hale raised his hand. "I'm well aware of what the Brotherhood Protectors can do for me in a case like this, but I'm not even close to being able to issue a search warrant, much less drag Vernon in for questioning. It's too early for that. I need time and more importantly, for you and your men to give me room to do my job."

"What the hell is that supposed to mean?" Waylen asked.

"Vernon knows you're tailing him and because of that, he's holed up in his house or places of business, lying low. How the hell am I supposed to catch him at his own game when he's refusing to play? Maybe if you gave him a little more rope—"

"No. No fucking way." Waylen shook his head.

"He blew up her boat and broke into her home. I'm not letting him come after her again."

"Look. You're with her twenty-four seven. You can protect her. Let me handle Vernon. Okay? Call off your men. Put them on the marina. The boats. I don't care, but I can't have them up Vernon's ass. It's hindering what I need to do to shut him down. There's more going on than what happened with Presley."

Waylen glanced toward the sky. A big, puffy white cloud danced across the sun. His father had taught him to respect the police. He'd given his entire life to serving his country. He'd worked with every government agency known to man. Most were good people, and he trusted his instincts. Hale was about as good as they came.

"How big is this case you're working on?" Waylen asked.

"Probably the biggest one of my career," Hale said. "Unfortunately, it's the kind of thing that takes time to put together." He glanced over his shoulder. "I shouldn't be telling you this, but two months ago, we put an undercover cop on the streets. His goal is to get inside an arms dealer organization. I just got word yesterday that he was supposed to meet with the head honcho. But it got canceled."

"You believe Vernon's that man?" Presley asked.

Hale stared at Presley but said nothing.

"Come on, Hale. I gave you all those financials.

You know as well as I do what that looks like. He was laundering money through Driftwood Tours. Possibly running drugs or guns. When Presley took over the books and divorced that asshole, that deal went away on him, and he had to scramble," Waylen said. "I've been nothing but straight with you. If you want me to call off my team, give me a damn good reason to. Otherwise, we'll do this my way."

"Fuck. I can't have that," Hale muttered. "Fine. Yeah. I looked closely at those records, and I agree. That's exactly what Vernon was doing. We believe he's doing that with his other businesses. And yeah, we believe he's buying and selling guns, among other things."

"Jesus," Presley whispered. "How did I not know any of this? I feel like the biggest fool."

"Hey. Don't beat yourself up." Hale reached out and squeezed her forearm. "You know my wife, Gina, right?"

Presley nodded.

"Do you know how I met her?"

"I heard the stories," Presley said.

"How do you think she felt when I busted down her door and arrested her husband for being a serial rapist? She had no idea. While she knew her husband had cheated on her, she had no clue he was the one going around taking advantage of teenage girls. It was a total shock and something she still grapples with. Even if you saw the signs, I know enough about your family history to know you had other things going on at that time."

"I'm sorry for what Gina had to go through. I don't wish that on anyone," Presley said softly.

"Men like Vernon find your vulnerabilities and exploit them. No one can protect themselves completely from that. Not even people like me and Waylen." Hale dropped his hand and shifted his gaze. "Are you going to call off your team?"

"On one condition," Waylen said. "I want daily updates. I want to be completely in the loop, and I want your word that you won't stop us from doing our own investigating."

Hale let out a long breath. "As long as it's not illegal, I won't stop you." He poked Waylen in the chest. "But you've already skirted that line a few times with this IT shit. Be careful. Don't put in a position where I can't use what you give me."

"Trust me, I know how this shit works." Waylen pulled out his cell. "I'll text my boys now. However, if Vernon comes after my girl, or any one of my men, all bets are off."

"I just hope I'm not putting handcuffs on you because I hate doing that to people I like." Hale turned and marched off toward his dark sedan.

"Are you really going to ask Raider and Harlan to stop following Vernon?" Presley asked.

"Yes and no." Waylen texted the team to inform

them of the situation. "I had Harlan slip into Vernon's house and bug it this morning. It's better than nothing."

"So, I'm a sitting duck."

He pulled her close to his chest. "Babe, Hale's right. We need to give Vernon rope to hang himself. You'll never be alone. I'll always be with you, and one of my team members will always be close by. If and when Vernon comes, he won't know what hit him. But let's hope Hale gets to him first, because I won't be using cuffs to take him down. I'll put him six feet under."

"Don't talk like that." She shoved him, placing her hand on her stomach. "I don't need you going to jail for being a Neanderthal."

His heart dropped to his toes. He glanced between her belly and her eyes. "Are you trying to tell me something?"

She planted her hands on her hips. "Yeah. Don't even joke about things that could send you to prison. I don't find it funny. I get you'll do whatever it takes to keep me safe, but I can't have you going all rogue on me or shooting off your mouth."

He inched closer, his mind spinning with thoughts that had nothing to do with Vernon and the threat that he posed. However, he did understand her concern about his words. "I'm not going to do anything to him unprovoked. While I've been in situations where human life has been lost because of my career, I don't take that lightly and I shouldn't have implied I'd do that so easily. I'm sorry for that. The only way that would happen is if he were to try to kill you, me, or any one of my men." He took her hand and pressed it against her midsection. "What I want to know is why did you do this when you got so upset with me about my poor choice of words?" He tilted his head. "It's like you were protecting something. Like a baby."

"It's a little too early to know about that." She pushed his hand away.

"Then why did you do it?"

"Because I felt sick to my stomach. We just found each other again, and if there's one thing I know about you, it's that you're fiercely protective of those you love. You'd do anything for them, including something crazy."

He palmed her cheek. "I do love you, and you're right. I'd lay down my life for you. But trust me when I say I won't do anything stupid." He kissed her tenderly. "Are you sure it's too soon to find out?"

"Positive. I'm not even late yet."

"You promise you'll tell me as soon as you get it or don't get it?"

"Yeah." She patted his shoulder. "Can we go? It's getting late and I'm hungry."

"Why don't we stop at that little Italian place you like and pick up something to bring back to the marina? Sound good?"

"Sounds great."

Waylen opened the door, helping her into the passenger seat. He jogged around the hood of the car. He didn't like not believing Presley, but he could tell she wasn't being completely truthful about the whole baby thing.

On the one hand, he totally believed she didn't know if she was pregnant. However, he could tell by the way she stared at him that she wondered if she could be.

The really scary part was that Waylen wanted her to have his kid. He wanted a family, a concept he'd given up on a long time ago.

13

_P_resley stared out the window. She'd gone through the calculations in her head a dozen times. Tomorrow she'd be a day late.

It didn't necessarily mean anything other than she would officially begin to worry. As if she wasn't already doing that.

Waylen reached across the vehicle and took her hand. "You haven't said a word since we stopped and picked up food. What's going on?"

"I'm tired," she said.

He kissed her palm. "I know you're concerned about me calling off the boys from tailing Vernon, but there's no way he's going to be able to get to you."

A million things ran through her mind, most of which didn't have to do with Vernon. She wanted him out of her family business and out of her life for good. Whatever it took to make that happen, she was on board with it. She trusted Waylen and his team, along with Hale. They were the experts, and she knew they would all eventually get the job done.

It was the sitting around and waiting for it to happen that made her crazy, but she didn't have a choice, not if she wanted Vernon to go away for good. Someone had to put a stop to his madness. She couldn't let him hurt anyone else.

She pulled her hand away. "I'm also still mad at you." She turned. When she'd admitted to Sally that she wanted Waylen to stay and had made the promise she'd tell Waylen how she felt, she hadn't realized what that would do to her heart. The confusion it would create in her mind and soul.

The past, present, and future collided like a tidal wave crashing into the shore.

"Why? What did I do now?"

Explaining it all would open up a can of worms that couldn't be closed, but it wouldn't be fair to either of them in the long run if she didn't. His mother and everyone had been right. She always put everyone else in front of herself and it was high time she stopped, even if it did break her heart.

"We're hanging on to what was, not what is," she said.

"What the hell is that supposed to mean?"

"You never let me go. You held on to every memory you had of me. It ruined your marriage."

"Oh no, you don't." He glanced in her direction with a hard glare. "When Elena found that box, our relationship was already dead."

"That may be true, but you were clinging to a part of the past and so was I. The day I married Vernon, I stood in front of a mirror in my wedding dress and my first thought was how much you would have hated that dress."

"I'm sure you looked beautiful in it." He rolled to a stop at a red light. They were still about eight miles from the marina.

"I did, but that doesn't change the fact that it wasn't the kind of gown I would have picked out if I was marrying you. It wasn't the kind of wedding we would have had, and that's what I was thinking about."

"What does this have to do with anything?" Waylen angrily punched the gas and then had to tap the brakes to avoid hitting the car in front of them.

She pressed her hand on the dashboard. "Both of us spent our adult lives pining over something we couldn't have. Maybe it's because we didn't get the opportunity to have proper closure. I don't know. It doesn't matter. But now that we've spent these two weeks together, we've eased into this comfortable thing like it was yesterday. It's not. We're different people and we can't keep acting like what we had is enough to jump into a life together. It's crazy. I know I said I wanted you to stay, and it's not that I don't want you to, because the idea of you leaving again hurts. However, I have to ask myself, why?"

"I think the answer is pretty simple."

"No, Waylen. Not if we're being completely honest. We're living in the past. We're thinking about all the things that could have been. All the things we could have done differently back then. It's weird. It's just as unhealthy as how we held on to each other during our adult lives."

He took a turn a little too aggressively, and she had to grab the holy shit bar. She wanted to yell at him about his driving but opted to keep her mouth shut about that. One argument at a time.

"You want a heavy dose of truth?" He slammed on the brakes at a stop sign and then gunned it. "I don't regret my life." He shifted his gaze and arched a brow. "Leaving here was a good thing for me and my mom. She needed to get off this island to grieve with her family. I'm not sure she could have gotten through it if she stayed. And if I'm being honest with myself, I couldn't have either. Being with my aunts, uncles, and cousins gave me a different perspective. A different view of my dad and his life. It was all very healing."

"I'm glad," she whispered.

"I won't deny how much I missed you or my friends back here on Big Island. But I forged ahead with my life. The Naval Academy. I worked my ass off and I'm proud of my accomplishments. Even my marriage to Elena, which was hell in the end, didn't start off as bad. And yeah, I thought about you, but who doesn't think about their first everything." He lifted his gaze, glancing in the rearview, then the side mirrors. "I don't find any of this strange. Or unhealthy, as you put it. And I'm sure as fuck not living in the past. I'm right here. In the moment, and if you can't see that, I'm unsure what to tell you." He shifted lanes and passed a vehicle.

"Jesus. What's wrong with you? Why are you driving like a madman?"

"I think someone's following us," he said. "Get my cell out of my back pocket." He lifted his ass.

She reached across the car and plucked it.

"Text the team group message. Mano's on it, too. Tell them I'm being followed and to track me. Also, tell them there are three cars on my tail, and I need backup." He reached across her and popped open the glove box, pulling out his weapon.

"I hate guns."

"I know, babe, but it's a necessary evil in some situations." He held his pistol on his lap while he weaved in and out of traffic.

"What else should I do?"

"Stay low and hold on."

The closer Waylen got to the marina, the heavier the traffic got.

His cell rang.

He tapped the CarPlay button. "Hey, Kian."

"I'm a mile from your location. Lane is behind me, and Mano is coming up behind you about half a mile away. Harlan and Raider stayed behind just in case Vernon has someone coming to the marina."

"Good call," Waylen said. "I've got three SUVs on my tail. One right on me. The other two are hanging about four cars back."

"What do you want to do?" Kian asked.

"Nothing in this traffic unless they force our hand," Waylen said.

"Mano thinks you should go to his place. It's a fortress. No one is getting in or out."

Waylen gripped his weapon. He sucked in a deep breath. "If we go there, we aren't getting out without being ambushed once we leave."

"That holds true at the marina, too," Kian said. "Have you been able to see any of the drivers?"

"No."

Presley popped her head up over the seat.

"Jesus. Get down." Waylen grabbed her shoulder.

"I was just trying to see if I recognized Vernon's car." She glared. "I doubt he's going to shoot me with a street full of witnesses."

"He tried to blow you up once already. I'm not

taking any chances." Waylen arched a brow. "I should have never let Hale talk me into pulling off the tail."

"I disagree," Kian said. "Now don't get pissed at what I'm about to suggest."

"I don't like it already." Waylen swallowed. He knew exactly where his buddy was about to go because he'd already thought it.

"We've already slowed down whatever Vernon was doing and—"

Hale's number appeared on the dash. "Kian, hang on. It's Hale. Let me see what he wants." Waylen tapped the CarPlay and accepted Hale's call while he turned down the side street heading toward the marina. "What's up, Hale?"

"It's Frank. He's awake and he's singing like a canary."

"What exactly does that mean?"

"It means we've got Vernon dead to rights," Hale said. "I had to cut a deal with Frank to do it, but I got the bastard on arms deals. Drug running. Money laundering. You name it, I got him. Frank wants to nail that asshole for trying to kill him."

"Does Frank know why?"

"Yeah. Vernon owes him money. Lots of it. First payment was due before that charter and Vernon talked Frank into taking it as a gift, putting him off for a couple of weeks. Now all I have to do is find the fucker since he knows Frank turned."

"How the hell does he know that?"

"He had a plant at the hospital. We didn't know that until they informed Vernon, who has now disappeared on us."

"I think I might know where he is, and I can help you with that, but you're not going to like it, and you're going to be late to the party."

"Shit," Hale mumbled. "What's happening?"

"Gather the troops and meet us at the marina. But don't come in guns blazing. Wait for a text from me or someone from my team. And you're going to have to let me and my men do this my way because Vernon and his men are already on my ass."

"Just don't make me arrest you, got it?"

"I'll do my best." Waylen tapped the screen. "Kian?"

"I'm here."

"Turn around and go back to the marina. We're going to bring these fuckers to us. He wants to play, let's show him how it's done."

"Are you sure you want to put Presley in the line of fire like that?" Kian asked.

He glanced at Presley, who tilted her head, staring at him with wide eyes. She blinked.

"I want him out of my life," she whispered.

"I'm sorry. I didn't want to do it this way, but I don't see another option. Do you think you can face him?"

She nodded.

"Get everyone ready. It's showtime." He ended the call and then took Presley's hand. "Whatever happens, you need to know three things. First, I love you. No doubt in my mind about that. Second. The past is long gone. I'm not living there and I wouldn't want to. And third, I might say some things that are hurtful, mean, and completely out of character when all this goes down. I'm doing it to get a rise out of Vernon. So if that happens, remember the first two things, okay?"

"As long as you don't believe anything Vernon has to say about me."

Waylen laughed. "I'll try not to."

14

*W*aylen pushed the comms into his ear. "Check. Check." He stood in the middle of the office with his heart hammering in his chest. He'd been in a million dangerous situations where his life had been on the line. The life of his men.

But he'd never had to protect the woman he loved.

This changed everything.

He reached into his pocket and fingered the piece of jewelry. This was a fucking crazy game he was playing. If he even got the chance to play it.

"Mano in place."

"Lane in place."

"Raider in place."

"Lane in overwatch. I've got all three cars in sight. I count eight men. Heavily armed."

"Kian in place."

"Harlan in place. I've got Vernon at the gate."

"These bastards won't know what hit them," Waylen said.

"They're dispersing. Two flanking north, heading in Raider's direction. Two heading around the south side through the alleyway," Lane said.

"I've got them," Harlan said.

"I see two coming down through the west," Mano said. "Once I take them out, I can double back and get the other two standing guard, but I'll need cover."

"I've got your back," Lane said.

"These assholes must really think we're idiots," Waylen muttered. He lifted Presley off the stool and gripped her by the shoulders. "You doing okay?"

"Hell no." She held his stare. "I'm about to be bait while you and your buddies are *taking out* gunmen. I'm fucking terrified."

"We're not killing them," he said. "Just immobilizing them while letting Vernon think he's got the upper hand."

"Doesn't make me feel any better."

"Time for you to get outside," Lane said over the comms.

"Come on. We better go for that nightly stroll." He opened the door and stepped outside, keeping her behind him, in case Vernon became trigger-happy.

They didn't make it more than five paces from the building before Vernon made his presence known.

"Hello, Presley. Waylen." Vernon's deep voice cut through the evening air like a wolf howling at the moon. He raised a weapon, pointing it directly at Waylen's chest.

Fucker.

"What the hell are you doing here?" Waylen asked. "You're not welcome."

"I don't give a shit." Vernon waved his gun. "Now both of you are coming with me."

"You're going to have to shoot me before that happens," Waylen said.

"Trust me, I will take great pleasure in doing that. But it will have to wait." He tapped his ear. "Call off your men. I know they're around here somewhere."

"Why would I do that?" Waylen asked.

"Because if you don't, mine will kill them and I don't think you want a bloodbath. Now, I'm being kind in letting them walk free. So either do as I say, or they all die."

Waylen tapped his ear. "Stand down." He might as well play along.

Vernon stretched out his free arm, wiggling his fingers. "Hand over your comms."

Fuck. Waylen didn't want to do that, but what

choice did he have? He plucked it from his ear and placed it in Vernon's palm.

"Now let's go." Vernon waved his weapon toward the docks.

Presley dug her fingers into Waylen's arm. "I'm not going anywhere with you. I'd rather fucking die first."

Jesus. Presley and her damn mouth.

"Sweetie, that's going to happen no matter what. Now start walking toward *Liberty*."

"And why are we doing that?" Waylen asked. He was flying blind. His team could no longer hear anything he said and no one was perched on the docks.

"You two lovebirds are going to have a little boating accident. Sad, but true." Vernon inched closer.

Waylen laughed. "Lovebirds? That's funny. No one is going to believe that. Not when I have a girlfriend back home."

Vernon tilted his head. "You expect me to fall for that? My wife has been hung up on you her entire life. You even called her your girlfriend. Not to mention, you've been hanging around her like a lovesick puppy. It's pathetic."

"You've totally misread this situation, man. I can't speak for Presley, but I left Big Island years ago and I've never looked back. I couldn't wait to get out of here and I certainly don't want to come back, much less get back with someone I had a thing with when I was seventeen. We had a nice little reunion. But it was a fling. That's all. I got sucked into a situation with the volcano and yeah, I stuck around to help her out because you're a dick. But she means nothing to me. Not like that anyway and my girlfriend wouldn't take too kindly to you implying otherwise."

"You're full of shit." Vernon aimed the gun at Waylen's head.

"I'm not." He held his hands up. "I was about to tell Presley that I was leaving tomorrow to go back to California so I could propose to my girlfriend. I was even going to show her the ring."

"You're buying for time, and it's a stupid cover story," Vernon said.

"Let me show you." Slowly, he reached into his pocket. He held his breath. Where the fuck were his men? They should have dealt with all the assholes by now. Gingerly, he took out his mother's engagement ring and held it up.

Presley peered over his shoulder and gasped.

Damn. His heart sank. The story was totally bogus. But that noise Presley made came right from her gut and broke his heart. Maybe she didn't believe the story, but she had to wonder why he had the ring.

Vernon took two steps closer, locking his gaze on the ring and that's all Waylen needed.

He shoved Presley to the ground and reached for Vernon's weapon, but the bastard was quick, and he jerked his arm back.

Waylen lunged forward. They wrestled to the ground.

Bang!

Presley screamed.

Waylen continued to roll around, tangled up with Vernon.

The gun had landed on the gravel and was currently out of reach.

He took a punch to his gut. He groaned, tossing a few of his own, reaching for the weapon. He curled his fingers around the handle.

Another fist to his shoulder.

Bang! Bang!

Footsteps clambered on the ground.

The sound of guns being cocked filled the air.

But it was too late. Vernon's limp body fell dead on top of Waylen.

Sirens wailed in the distance.

Waylen shoved him to the side.

Kian came up from behind, grabbing him and hoisting him to his feet.

Waylen shook out his hands. "I didn't really want to shoot the—"

"Waylen." Kian's hand came firmly down on his shoulder. "It's Presley. She's hurt."

"What!" Waylen spun on his heel. He raced to

Presley, who sat on the ground, holding her shoulder. "Babe, what happened?" Blood trickled through her fingers.

"It's a graze." She lifted her hand. "When the gun discharged, the bullet hit my shoulder."

"Shit. I'm so sorry." He ripped off his shirt and pressed it against the wound. It wasn't life-threatening, but still. His girl got hurt and it was his fault.

"Here. Your girlfriend might still want this." Presley held up his mother's engagement ring.

He chuckled. "Don't you remember the three things I told you in the car?"

"Yeah. But that was still pretty fucked up, and why do you have that thing anyway?"

This wasn't the time or the place. There were so many things to discuss. He needed to prove to Presley that he was indeed still the man for her and that he wasn't staying out of any sense of obligation or nostalgia. He took the ring and tucked it in his pocket. "That's a long story and I'll tell you all about it after we get you checked out at the hospital."

"That's not necessary."

He lifted her in his arms. "I'm going to be a Neanderthal and not take no for an answer."

She rested her head against his shoulder. "Thank you."

"For what?"

"Saving me. Again."

"That's kind of what boyfriends do."

As it turned out, Presley needed eight stitches. She lay back on the hospital bed with her legs crossed at her ankles and waited for the doctor to come back with her other request.

She'd sent Waylen to go find her a cheeseburger and fries. Hopefully the doc would come back first.

The curtain opened and the ER doctor appeared with a clipboard in hand. "How are you feeling?"

"My shoulder feels like someone shot me and then stuck me with a very large needle."

The doctor laughed. "I love a patient with a good sense of humor."

Presley shifted. "Do you have the results of that test I asked you to run?"

"I do," the doc said. "Would you like to wait for that handsome man who has been running around here with his head cut off like a chicken, barking orders at everyone, making sure we take proper care of you?"

"No. I was hoping to find out before he came back."

"All right." The doctor nodded. "It's very early, but you are pregnant."

Tears filled Presley's eyes. She'd fantasied about

this moment her entire life. But now that it was a reality, she had no idea how she really felt, except she knew without a doubt she wanted this baby.

And she wanted Waylen.

"I can't tell if this is good news or not." The doctor took her hand.

"A lot has happened tonight. I'm just overwhelmed," she managed.

"I can certainly understand that." The doctor squeezed her hand. "I will prescribe some prenatal vitamins. If you don't have an OB, I can recommend one. I do suggest you make an appointment with one as soon as possible."

"I have a good one, so I'll do that first thing in the morning."

"Good." The doctor nodded. "If you need anything at all, don't hesitate to reach out."

The sound of footsteps in the hallway echoed in her ears.

Waylen stepped into the room carrying a tray of food.

"I'll leave you two alone while I go start on your discharge papers. It will take a little bit. Enjoy your meal." The doctor ducked out of the room.

"Hey, you." Waylen set the tray on the table. "I was able to find everything you asked for."

"Thanks."

"I want you to know that my intention wasn't to end Vernon's life. I may not have had a good opinion of the man, but I never take pride in taking human life. It sucks, actually."

"I know." She snagged a fry and dunked it in ketchup. "I wanted him out of my life and I got my wish. It's just, no matter how hard I try to reconcile it in my head, he was still a human being."

"Who tried to kill you. Don't forget that."

"I haven't and he could have killed you, so I'm grateful that didn't happen."

"Me too," he said. "Now, there are a couple of other things we need to discuss."

That was putting it mildly. "Agreed, and I want to go first."

"Nope," he said. "I listened to you rant in the car before all this started and I didn't get a real chance to respond."

"Um, yeah, you did with your three things to remember." She arched a brow. "And then you went on and on about some girlfriend."

He groaned. "The only girlfriend I have is you, and you're going to let me say my piece, and then you can tell me whatever is on your mind." He lifted another fry and stuffed it in her mouth.

"Hey. That's not nice."

"Too bad," he said.

"I really hate it when you get like this," she mumbled. "But okay. I'm listening."

"I resented you telling me I was pining after you for all these years. And to be honest, it bothers me to think that you did. I want to believe that we went on with our lives, living them the best we could. That our memories brought us joy, not suffering."

"Waylen, they did. That's not what I meant."

"That's what it sounded like."

"All I wanted was to make sure you don't want you to stay because of what could have been. Or out of obligation."

"I'm not. On either account. I want to stay because of what is and I believe will be." He stuffed his hand in his pocket and pulled out his mother's engagement ring. "You know, I had to beg my mom for this ring when I planned on proposing to Elena. She never believed she was the one. She always had her reservations about Elena. And not because she didn't believe I didn't love her or even that Elena didn't love me. My mom didn't think it was the kind of love that could endure the test of time."

"Why are you telling me this?"

"My mother always wanted this ring to stay in the family. She wanted it on the finger of the one woman who made my heart sing. When you told me that our love was only based in the past, I saw red because part of me knew that was true, and I didn't want to face that reality."

Presley pressed her hand over her stomach. Her heart sank.

"But is that such a bad thing? Our love has stood the test of time. There isn't anyone I'd rather spend the rest of my life loving. There isn't anyone else out there for me. I went to that pawn shop and repurchased this ring so my mom would always have it. However, when I packed up to come to Big Island, she had me bring two things. My father's ashes and this ring. I get why she wanted me to take my dad's ashes. That's easy. I know exactly what she wants me to do with those. But for the life of me, I couldn't figure out why it was so important to her for me to carry this thing with me. But now I get it." He lifted her hand and placed it on her finger. "I understand if you don't want to wear it. I mean, it does have a weird history, but I love you and this belongs to you."

"Jesus. Are you trying to ask me to marry you?"

"Yeah. Something like that."

"That's the most fucked-up proposal I've ever heard." She held up her shaky hand and stared at the modest diamond gracing her finger. It was the most beautiful thing she'd ever seen. And it fit her perfectly.

"So, what do you think? You want to marry this old fool?"

"That all depends." She palmed his cheek. "Are you ready to be a dad?" She winced.

"A what now?" He jerked his head.

"I had the doctor run a blood test. It came back positive for a little Waylen."

"We are not naming any child, boy or girl,

Waylen." He cupped her face and kissed her, hard. "A baby? Seriously?"

"I wouldn't joke about something like that, but I love the name Waylen."

"Absolutely not. No juniors. And it's not a girl's name."

"It could be." She smiled. "We could call her Way-Way."

"You're not winning this one, Presley." He lifted her cheeseburger and took a massive bite. "I'm going to be a daddy. Hot diggity. Wait until the boys hear this one."

"I'd like to keep it quiet for now. I'm barely knocked up."

"Yes, dear."

She snagged the burger from his hands. "And don't ever eat a pregnant woman's food again. Not unless you want to get hurt *and* sleep on the sofa."

He waved his hands. "I can't wait to see you get all round and plump."

"Oh, that's mean."

"You know, you haven't answered my question yet." He lifted her hand and kissed it.

"I'll marry you on one condition."

"This should be good." He laughed.

"It's a small wedding. I don't have any family left, so just a few friends. Nothing fancy. No frills. No church. I want it on the water. And the honeymoon has to be on Mano's yacht."

"Done."

"All before I get fat."

"We can do it as soon as I can get my mom out here." He reached for a fry, but she batted his hand away.

"Get your own. I'm eating for two."

"Now who's being mean."

"I love you," she whispered.

"I love you too."

She'd waited a lifetime to have her dreams come true. But Waylen was well worth it.

15

Waylen lifted his coffee and sipped, glancing around the table. His heart swelled with love and pride. He'd gotten zero hours of sleep and didn't care. He'd crash soon enough. The night's events deserved a bit of a celebration.

Even if it came in the form of pancakes and coffee.

He smiled.

Lane had his arm draped over the back of Cassie's chair. Raider held Piper's hand, and Harlan whispered something into Storm's ear. Four out of five of his men had found something other than a great vacation, a little adventure, and the possibility of a new career on Big Island.

And he couldn't be happier for them.

Now if he could get Kian to get some game on and ask Blake out.

Presley squeezed his leg. "Thank you." She leaned in and kissed his cheek.

"For what?"

"Doing that interview and talking your friends into agreeing to do it as well."

He shrugged. "It's the least I could do after telling Lane and Kian about our little secret."

She jerked her head back. "You didn't?"

"Come on. As if you didn't tell Blake." He arched a brow.

"That's different."

"I don't see how." He lifted her chin with his thumb and kissed her sweet lips. He'd never tire of this. For the first time in a long while, a full picture of the future formed in his head.

A home with the only woman he ever loved. A cat, which wasn't exactly what he had planned on having as a pet, but it made Presley happy. Therefore, it made him happy.

A family.

And in the place that he'd always wanted to come back to.

Life didn't get any sweeter.

Kian tossed a napkin at him. "Break it up over there. You two are disgusting."

"You're just jealous." Waylen reached into his water glass, snagged an ice cube, and chucked it at Kian.

"Asshole," Kian muttered.

"So, when's the wedding?" Blake asked.

"We're thinking next month if we can pull it off," Presley said. "And as long as his mom can find a place and get here."

"Exciting times." Harlan raised his glass. "Here's to Waylen and Presley. May you always have us at your side."

The entire table burst out laughing.

Waylen's life had come full circle. Just like his father had always told him it would.

Presley rested her hand on his thigh. "He would be proud of you," she whispered as if she knew exactly what he was thinking.

"And your parents would be proud of you." He smiled.

"They're all toasting us from the heavens," Presley said. "My dad always had faith that you'd return and that we'd be together. I wish I had believed him."

"According to my father, timing was everything. Patience was never our strong suit, but here we are. This is our time and I will enjoy growing old with you."

Presley bit her nails while she patiently waited for Waylen to finish the article, which focused on Waylen's return to Big Island, the water rescue and subsequent problems with Vernon until the show-down at the marina, and the second chance love story between her and Waylen.

It wasn't an interview Waylen, or any of his buddies, wanted anything to do with.

But Waylen ultimately relented when it meant good publicity for Driftwood Tours. After every-thing Vernon had done, she needed all the decent press she could get.

And his buddies didn't need any of their arms twisted. They stepped up to the plate without having to be asked.

Waylen set the paper aside and shifted on the bed, adjusting the covers.

"Well, what do you think?" she asked.

"I can't believe you gave them our prom picture." He arched a brow. "There were so many other pictures of us on the boats. Or hanging on the beach. That one you picked is fucking cheesy."

"I gave them five from when we were kids. That's the one they chose."

"I wouldn't have given them a choice." He tucked her hair behind her ears. "The article was good. Honestly, I enjoyed it and I think it will help with business."

"It wasn't too personal?"

"That was the point." He kissed her cheek. "I don't have a problem with anything the reporter said. It highlights all the key points. It talks a lot about your parents—my dad—all the stuff that will make people curious and book charters."

"And you don't think that will put us on display?"

He sucked in a deep breath and let it out slowly. "It might a little. However, eventually, it will die down. But hopefully it will be enough to get the business back on track."

"Do you really want to run fishing and scuba charters for me?"

"I have to do something." He shrugged. "And even when we do hammer out a deal with the Brotherhood Protectors, which I'm confident we will, it's not like I'm going to be on assignment every day. I'll have a fair amount of downtime, and that concept will make my skin crawl. About the only thing that made retirement bearable was fishing and trust me when I say my team hated every second of every fishing charter I roped them into. I'll love it." He rested his hand on her stomach. "Besides, the bigger you get, the harder it will become for you to do some of these things."

"You better not become one of those husbands who acts like I'm incapable of doing shit because I'm pregnant. I plan on working right up until I go into labor."

"I have this weird feeling we'll be arguing about this one for the next eight months."

She laughed, resting her head on his shoulder. "That and this kiddo's name."

"I'm not giving my child my name. It's honestly too weird after you named a boat and a cat after me."

Way-Way jumped up on the bed, as if he knew they were discussing him, and stretched before snuggling up between Waylen's legs.

He picked up the cat, setting him on the kitty bed on the floor. "But I have been thinking about baby names."

"Oh really?" She tilted her head. "This should be interesting."

"If it's a boy, we could name him after our fathers."

She sat up taller. "Oh." Her heart swelled. Tears dribbled down her cheeks. "What would be the first name?"

"I thought we'd use your dad's name first since it's my father's surname that's being carried on."

"Nico Marlin Brown," she whispered, glancing up toward the ceiling. "Yeah. I like that."

"And if it's a girl, we flip it, using my mom's name first. Sally Victoria Brown. I know Sally's an old-fashioned name, but it was also my grandma and great-grandmother's."

"Waylen, I love that idea." She straddled his legs, resting her hands on his shoulders. "And I love you. Now all we need is a house for your mama and one for us. One that we can afford and everything I've looked at this morning is way too expensive."

He snagged his cell from the nightstand. "There's a place for sale in a neighborhood between here and that bar the boys and I like to hang out in. It's got an in-law apartment. We'll need babysitting and my mom comes free." He tapped away on his fingers and showed her the house.

She knew exactly the one he was talking about. She took the phone and swallowed. The house was perfect. The apartment was behind the pool. It was a spacious one-bedroom and had everything his mom could need.

The house itself had four bedrooms with a master downstairs. It had the most gorgeous kitchen, which was open to a great room. The location was fifteen to twenty minutes from every place she could possibly want to be.

It was perfect.

Except the price.

"Do you have a problem with my mom staying that close?" Waylen asked.

"No. Not at all. But how the hell can we afford that?"

"I have some money saved." He took the cell and set it aside. "Between that and you now owning this business free and clear, we have enough to make that happen, especially with a free nanny."

"Are you sure? That seems—"

He pressed his finger over her lips. "We have some things to discuss, including my finances. I'm not rich, but I'm not poor either. Tomorrow, we'll go through what I've got because that all becomes ours. We'll make a plan for our family's future, and if we both think we can swing that house, then next week, we'll go put an offer on it."

Her eyes welled with tears.

She turned.

"Hey." He cupped her face. "Why are you crying?"

"I don't know. Maybe it's hormones. Or maybe it's that I have to keep pinching myself." She held his stare. "I used to sit back and watch people I thought had happy marriages. My parents. Your parents. Mano's folks. Remi and Aleka. Lisa and Al. The one thing they all had in common was no division of possessions. No, this is mine, and that's yours, especially with Mano's mom and dad. His father came from nothing. He didn't have two pennies to rub together, yet his mom gave him the keys to the castle."

"Mano's parents loved each other very much. It took a while for his grandparents to get on board, but they supported it when they realized he wasn't marrying her for money."

She slid down next to Waylen, hugging him close. "You should know I'm only marrying you for your good looks and the fact that you're great in bed."

"Ditto," Waylen said. "I love you."

"I love you too." She closed her eyes and let her body relax. She couldn't look back on the last twenty-three years and wish them away. Being with Waylen was her destiny, but in order for her to be with the man she was born to love, she had to live through everything else.

Or they would have never gotten to this point.

Nothing in her life had been a mistake.

Nothing.

And now she finally had everything she'd ever dreamed of. Her father had been right. Waylen was not only worth the wait, but he was also the ship she would sail away with on her forever journey.

Brotherhood Protectors Hawaii World Team Koa Alpha

Lane Unleashed - Regan Black

Harlan Unleashed - Stacey Wilk

Raider Unleashed - Lori Matthews

Waylen Unleashed - Jen Talty

Kian Unleashed - Kris Norris

Thank you for taking the time to read *Waylen Unleashed*. Please feel free to leave an honest review.

If you want to learn more about Darius Ford, check out: ***Darius' Promise***

Grab a glass of vino, kick back, relax, and let the romance roll in…

Sign up for my .Newsletter (https://dl.bookfunnel.com/ 82gm8b9k4y) where I often give away free books before publication.

Join my private Facebook group (https://www.facebook. com/groups/191706547909047/) where I post exclusive excerpts and discuss all things murder and love!

ABOUT THE AUTHOR

Jen Talty is the *USA Today* Bestselling Author of Contemporary Romance, Romantic Suspense, and Paranormal Romance. In the fall of 2020, her short story was selected and featured in a 1001 Dark Nights Anthology.

Regardless of the genre, her goal is to take you on a ride that will leave you floating under the sun with warmth in your heart. She writes stories about broken heroes and heroines who aren't necessarily looking for romance, but in the end, they find the kind of love books are written about :).

She first started writing while carting her kids to one hockey rink after the other, averaging 170 games per year between 3 kids in 2 countries and 5 states. Her first book, IN TWO WEEKS was originally published in 2007. In 2010 she helped form a publishing company (Cool Gus Publishing) with *NY Times* Bestselling Author Bob Mayer where she ran the technical side of the business through 2016.

Jen is currently enjoying the next phase of her life…
the empty nester! She and her husband reside in
Jupiter, Florida.

Grab a glass of vino, kick back, relax, and let the
romance roll in…

*Sign up for my Newsletter (https://dl.bookfunnel.com/
82gm8b9k4y) where I often give away free books before
publication.*

*Join my private Facebook group (https://www.facebook.
com/groups/191706547909047/) where I post exclusive
excerpts and discuss all things murder and love!*

Never miss a new release. Follow me on
Amazon:amazon.com/author/jentalty

And on Bookbub: bookbub.com/authors/jen-
talty

ALSO BY JEN TALTY

Brand new series: SAFE HARBOR!

Mine To Keep

Mine To Save

Mine To Protect

Mine to Hold

Mine to Love

Check out LOVE IN THE ADIRONDACKS!

Shattered Dreams

An Inconvenient Flame

The Wedding Driver

Clear Blue Sky

Blue Moon

Before the Storm

NY STATE TROOPER SERIES (also set in the Adirondacks!)

In Two Weeks

Dark Water

Deadly Secrets

Murder in Paradise Bay

Searching for Haven

DELTA FORCE-NEXT GENERATION

Shielding Jolene

Shielding Aalyiah

Shielding Laine

Shielding Talullah

Shielding Maribel

Shielding Daisy

The Men of Thief Lake

Rekindled

Destiny's Dream

Federal Investigators

Jane Doe's Return

The Butterfly Murders

THE AEGIS NETWORK

The Sarich Brother

The Lighthouse

Her Last Hope

The Last Flight

The Return Home

The Matriarch

Rough Beauty

The Brotherhood Protectors
The Saving Series
Saving Love
Saving Magnolia
Saving Leather

Hot Hunks
Cove's Blind Date Blows Up
My Everyday Hero – Ledger
Tempting Tavor
Malachi's Mystic Assignment
Needing Neor

Holiday Romances
A Christmas Getaway
Alaskan Christmas
Whispers
Christmas In The Sand

Heroes & Heroines on the Field
Taking A Risk
Tee Time

BROTHERHOOD PROTECTORS WORLD

ORIGINAL SERIES BY ELLE JAMES

Brotherhood Protectors Hawaii World

Team Koa Alpha

Lane Unleashed - Regan Black

Harlan Unleashed - Stacey Wilk

Raider Unleashed - Lori Matthews

Waylen Unleashed - Jen Talty

Kian Unleashed - Kris Norris

Brotherhood Protectors Yellowstone World

Team Wolf

Guarding Harper - - Desiree Holt

Guarding Hannah - Delilah Devlin

Guarding Eris - Reina Torres

Guarding Payton - Jen Talty

Guarding Leah - Regan Black

Team Eagle

Booker's Mission - Kris Norris

Hunter's Mission - Kendall Talbot

Gunn's Mission - Delilah Devlin

Xavier's Mission - Lori Matthews

Wyatt's Mission - Jen Talty

Corbin's Mission - Jen Talty

Tyson's Mission - Delilah Devlin

Knox's Mission - Barb Han

Colton's Mission - Kendall Talbot

Walker's Mission - Kris Norris

Brotherhood Protectors Colorado World

Team Watchdog

Mason's Watch - Jen Talty

Asher's Watch - Leanne Tyler

Cruz's Watch - Stacey Wilk

Kent's Watch- Deanna L. Rowley

Ryder's Watch- Kris Norris

Team Raptor

Darius' Promise - Jen Talty

Simon's Promise - Leanne Tyler

Nash's Promise - Stacey Wilk

Spencer's Promise - Deanna L. Rowley

Logan's Promise - Kris Norris

Team Falco

Fighting for Esme - Jen Talty

Fighting for Charli - Leanne Tyler

Fighting for Tessa - Stacey Wilk

Fighting for Kora - Deanna L. Rowley

Fighting for Fiona - Kris Norris

Athena Project

Beck's Six - Desiree Holt

Victoria's Six - Delilah Devlin

Cygny's Six - Reina Torres

Fay's Six - Jen Talty

Melody's Six - Regan Black

Team Trojan

Defending Sophie - Desiree Holt

Defending Evangeline - Delilah Devlin

Defending Casey - Reina Torres

Defending Sparrow - Jen Talty

Defending Avery - Regan Black

BROTHERHOOD PROTECTORS

ORIGINAL SERIES BY ELLE JAMES

Brotherhood Protectors International

Athens Affair (#1)

Belgian Betrayal (#2)

Croatia Collateral (#3)

Dublin Debacle (#4)

Edinburgh Escape (#5)

Brotherhood Protectors Hawaii

Kalea's Hero (#1)

Leilani's Hero (#2)

Kiana's Hero (#3)

Maliea's Hero (#4)

Emi's Hero (#5)

Sachie's Hero (#6)

Kimo's Hero (#7)

Alana's Hero (#8)

Nala's Hero (#9)

Mika's Hero (#10)

Bayou Brotherhood Protectors

Remy (#1)

Gerard (#2)

Lucas (#3)

Beau (#4)

Rafael (#5)

Valentin (#6)

Landry (#7)

Simon (#8)

Maurice (#9)

Jacques (#10)

Brotherhood Protectors Yellowstone

Saving Kyla (#1)

Saving Chelsea (#2)

Saving Amanda (#3)

Saving Liliana (#4)

Saving Breely (#5)

Saving Savvie (#6)

Saving Jenna (#7)

Saving Peyton (#8)

Saving Londyn (#9)

Brotherhood Protectors Colorado

SEAL Salvation (#1)

Brotherhood Protectors

ABOUT ELLE JAMES

ELLE JAMES also writing as MYLA JACKSON is a *New York Times* and *USA Today* Bestselling author of books including cowboys, intrigues and paranormal adventures that keep her readers on the edges of their seats. When she's not at her computer, she's traveling, snow skiing, boating, or riding her ATV, dreaming up new stories. Learn more about Elle James at www.ellejames.com

Website | Facebook | Twitter | GoodReads | Newsletter | BookBub | Amazon

Or visit her alter ego Myla Jackson at mylajackson.com
Website | Facebook | Twitter | Newsletter

Follow Me!
www.ellejames.com
ellejamesauthor@gmail.com

Made in the USA
Coppell, TX
31 October 2024

39415640R00164